Just as she was thinking the kiss might never end—and hoping it wouldn't—he pulled away.

"I—I need to take care of something," he said, turning away and striding to the door. Without another word, he was gone.

Carly stared after him. What had she done?

Stunned, she made her way slowly to the sofa on legs that would barely hold her and sank onto it.

Maybe the question she needed to ask herself was why she wanted to kiss him so badly. Part of the answer was easy. His kisses made her forget her problems. But kissing him—even wanting to kiss him—only made the problems worse. Fleeing her wedding with no plan for her future proved how impulsive she was. Falling for Dev—

No. She hadn't fallen for him yet.

Or had she?

Dear Reader,

April is an exciting month for the romance industry because that is when our authors learn whether or not their titles have been nominated for the prestigious RITA® Award sponsored by the Romance Writers of America. As with the Oscars, our authors will find out whether they've actually won in a glamorous evening event that caps off the RWA national conference in July. Of course, all the Silhouette Romance titles this month are already winners to me!

Karen Rose Smith heads up this month's lineup with her tender romance *To Protect and Cherish* (#1810) in which a cowboy-at-heart bachelor becomes a father overnight. *Prince Incognito* (#1811) by Linda Goodnight features another equally unforgettable hero—this one a prince masquerading as an ordinary guy. Nearly everyone accepts his disguise except, of course, our perceptive heroine who is now torn between the dictates of her head…and her heart. Longtime Silhouette Romance author Sharon De Vita returns with *Doctor's Orders* (#1812), in which a single mother who has been badly burned by love discovers a handsome doctor just might have the perfect prescription for her health and longtime happiness. Finally, in Roxann Delaney's *His Queen of Hearts* (#1813), a runaway bride goes from the heat and into the fire when she finds herself holed up in a remote location with her handsome rescuer.

Happy reading!
Sincerely,

Ann Leslie Tuttle
Associate Senior Editor

Please address questions and book requests to:
Silhouette Reader Service
U.S.: 3010 Walden Ave., P.O. Box 1325, Buffalo, NY 14269
Canadian: P.O. Box 609, Fort Erie, Ont. L2A 5X3

His Queen
of Hearts
Roxann Delaney

SILHOUETTE *Romance*®

Published by Silhouette Books

America's Publisher of Contemporary Romance

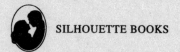

SILHOUETTE BOOKS

ISBN 0-373-19813-2

HIS QUEEN OF HEARTS

Copyright © 2006 by Roxann Delaney

This edition published by arrangement with Harlequin Books S.A.

® and TM are trademarks of Harlequin Books S.A., used under license. Trademarks indicated with ® are registered in the United States Patent and Trademark Office, the Canadian Trade Marks Office and in other countries.

Visit Silhouette Books at www.eHarlequin.com

Printed in U.S.A.

Books by Roxann Delaney

Silhouette Romance

Rachel's Rescuer #1509
A Saddle Made for Two #1533
A Whole New Man #1658
The Truth About Plain Jane #1748
His Queen of Hearts #1813

ROXANN DELANEY

doesn't remember a time when she wasn't reading or writing, and she always loved that touch of romance in both. A native Kansan, she's lived on a farm and in a small town, and has now returned to live in the city where she was born. Her four daughters and grandchildren keep her busy when she isn't writing, designing Web sites or planning her high school class reunions. The 1999 Maggie Award winner is thrilled to have followed the yellow brick road to the land of Silhouette Romance and loves to hear from readers. Contact her at roxann@roxanndelaney.com. Also be sure to visit her Web site at www.roxanndelaney.com.

To Allison Lyons, one of Silhouette's best, for her hard work and dedication in keeping me on track. I couldn't have done it without you! And to Hazel Dalbom, my high school English teacher, who not only taught but also encouraged both good writing and creativity.

Chapter One

Devon Brannigan tugged at the black leather patch covering his left eye and tried to find a more comfortable position on the hard church pew. He couldn't believe his good luck. In only a matter of time, he would finally have his hands on his no-good, greedy former neighbor. Once J.R.'s wedding vows were spoken, and the newlyweds departed for the reception, not only Dev but his two brothers back home would taste the sweetness of revenge.

Ignoring the choking scent of flowers that filled the sanctuary of the Baton Rouge church, he settled in for what he hoped would be a short wait. But he could wait as long as he had to. If nothing else, he was a patient and thorough man. He'd been trailing J.R. for months, always missing him by minutes. This time it wouldn't happen. This time J.R. would be stopped from conning any more innocent people and would pay for his crimes.

The organ music rose to a crescendo and then slowly came to a close. Dev folded his arms on his chest, more than willing to enjoy J.R.'s last moments as a free man. The thought made him chuckle to himself. Marriage wouldn't be the only bonds holding James Robert Staton when everything had played out. Dev wanted every penny owed him, but, even more, he wanted the man behind bars. Once the couple was on their way to their honeymoon hideaway, it would take one call to the authorities, and the Feds would take care of J.R. He chuckled again and earned a warning stare from the plump, middle-aged woman beside him. Turning to her, he smiled, knowing what her reaction would be to the look in his one eye and the patch over the other. With a huff of air, she faced forward, her shoulders bunched in indignation, exactly as he expected.

As the droning of the minister's voice continued, Dev focused his attention on the ceremony. Staring at the back of the groom only made him more eager to get this rolling, and since there was nothing he could do about that, he let his gaze slide over the bride. Not that he could see that much of her. If he'd known anything about fashion, he might have admired her wedding dress. But to him it was nothing more than a shroud of white covering what might or might not be a delightful body. It didn't matter. He had better things to do than chase after women.

But he couldn't ignore the perfection of her profile when she turned to smile at her groom. J.R. might be considered a handsome man, but he didn't deserve the beauty he'd soon be wed to. Did she deserve the shock she'd be in for as soon as the I do's were said?

Before Dev could imagine how distraught the bride might become when he played his hand and how she might just throw in a wild card he hadn't considered, she faced the guests. Enchanted by the vision of the auburn-haired beauty, Dev barely heard her clear her throat, intent on the nervous smile playing at her full lips.

"Thank you all for coming to share this special day," she said, her husky voice wobbling slightly. "I want to thank my mama for this beautiful wedding. And my bridesmaids for all their loving support."

Dev wasn't sure if her gesture was customary, but by the wary look in J.R.'s eyes, he knew something unplanned was happening. Uncrossing his arms, he sat up straighter, still hoping to remain unnoticed, yet wishing he had a better view.

The bride's gaze darted from one side of the church to the other. J.R. reached out to take her hand, but she pulled back, bestowing him with a trembling smile, and looked directly at one of the women in the wedding party. "I'd especially like to thank my maid of honor, Priscilla. She probably isn't aware of it, but she did me a great service two nights ago by sleeping with James."

A collective gasp rose among the guests, followed by silence and then a quiet murmur that grew louder. A spattering of giggles could be heard near the front of the church where J.R. stood like a marble statue, never batting an eye. The maid of honor turned to glance at the guests, her face pale. As bright spots of color appeared on her cheeks, her mouth opened, but nothing came out.

"It's all right, Prissy," the bride told her. "It really is." She smiled, her eyes glittering, and looked down at a woman on the end of the front row. "I'm sorry, Mama, but I can't do this. I just can't."

Gathering her voluminous skirt, she nearly flew up the aisle. For a moment there was no sound, and then an anguished cry from the woman she'd spoken to filled the crowded room. "You have to, Carolyn!"

The rustle of lace swept past Dev. Acting on instinct, Devon slammed his Stetson on his head and jumped to his feet, hurrying to catch her by one lace-covered elbow as she pushed open the massive wooden door. Sunlight blinded him for a moment, but he held tight to her to keep her from stumbling.

"God help me," he heard her whisper.

He tugged his hat farther down as a shield from the sunshine and prying eyes. "Well, I'm sure not God, sugar, but I'll be more than happy to do whatever I can," he replied, guiding her down the steps.

She didn't fight him as he hustled her toward his Jeep, parked less than half a block away. The click of her heels on the sidewalk echoed with each step, until they heard the church doors burst open and the sound of agitated voices behind them. Reaching his vehicle, Dev yanked open the passenger door for her and waited until she bunched her dress enough to slide in. Then he circled the front of the Jeep and climbed in behind the wheel.

Checking for traffic, he started the engine. "Hang on, sugar," he said, twisting the steering wheel to leave the parking spot with a squeal of rubber. He made a tight U-turn and stomped the accelerator just as they passed the growing crowd of people on the church steps. With a quick glance in that direction, he saw J.R. near the door, his hands fisted at his sides and a deep frown marring his good looks.

Gotcha. Dev smiled to himself. Things sure hadn't worked out as he'd planned, but he'd played the surprise hand he'd been dealt with his usual talent. Satisfied, he eased off on the gas and sneaked a look at his passenger.

Head tilted back to lean against the headrest and eyes closed, she was the perfect picture of a serene bride. But she couldn't be. She'd just jilted her groom at the altar. Any woman who'd been through what she must have couldn't be feeling calm.

"You okay?" he asked.

After a brief moment she nodded.

He glanced down at her hands. Knotted tightly in her lap, they gave her away. He was an expert at reading body language in his business and in everyday life, too. His thirty-four years had taught him well. He would let her calm down and get her thoughts together, and then he'd find out what was going on. Were J.R.'s cheating ways the only reason she'd dumped him, or was there more to it?

She didn't know it, but Dev had a stake in this. And she'd become his ace in the hole.

When her heart stopped slamming against her ribs and her body ceased trembling, Carly Albright took a deep breath and slowly let it out. How had she done it? Of course there'd been no choice, but how had she stood there and announced that she couldn't marry James? What would he do? What would her mama do?

So many questions and no answers. Maybe that was a good thing. If she could just put the incident out of her mind and— And what? She didn't even know where she was going, let alone how to deal with life once she got there.

And what must this man beside her, who'd blessedly come to her rescue, think of her?

She opened her eyes and peeked at him from under her lashes. For one second she couldn't breathe. Mercy goodness, but he was handsome! Dark, nearly ebony hair curled beneath the brim of his black cowboy hat. He wasn't dressed in western clothing, but something about him other than the hat shouted "cowboy." His jaw was strong, angular, his nose long and straight. High cheekbones gave him a European air, while a silvery scar ran across the bridge of his nose and disappeared on the other side. And those lips! Firm, yet full. Sensual. Carly had to press her own lips together to capture her sigh before it escaped.

He had a dangerous look about him, but she didn't feel threatened. In fact, she felt more secure than she had for weeks, ever since she'd started having doubts about marrying James.

Well, what's done is done, she thought, opening her eyes wide and lifting her hands to slip out the hairpins that held her headpiece. She'd find a way to make the best of it. She only hoped it didn't become a disaster, like her wedding.

"Do you mind if I toss this in the back?" she asked, pulling the multitiered veil off her head.

He didn't turn to look at her. "Be my guest."

Pivoting in the seat to stuff the netting in the back, she checked behind them to make sure no one was following. When she was satisfied that the highway behind them was clear of any familiar vehicles, she settled back into the seat again.

There was no sense worrying about it. It was done and over with. The only thing that worried her was her mama. But somehow, Carly knew Lily Mae Charpentier Albright would make out just fine. Maybe even better, if she went on with the plans they'd made about selling the mansion. Just as she would, herself. If only she *had* a plan.

"So. Where are we headed?" she asked over the muted strains of country music playing on the radio.

For a moment she thought he hadn't heard her. "Where can I drop you?" he finally asked. When she didn't answer, he glanced at her. "At home? A friend's? Relative's?"

Going home was out of the question. At least for now. The chance was too big that James would look for her there. She couldn't face him. And seeing family and friends would be more than humiliating. She felt bad about leaving her mama to deal with the backlash, but Mama could handle it with her usual Southern grace. Carly just wasn't up to it.

She looked down at her hands, tightly fisted in her lap. "I don't know," she answered honestly. "You were there. You saw what happened."

He was silent again, until a smile lifted the corner of his mouth. "Maybe you need some time. Would you like to go somewhere they can't find you?"

She really hadn't given it any thought, concentrating only on the wedding and how to stop it. "Well, yes, I guess I do."

"Thought so. I saw you checking to make sure we're not being followed. You can rest easy. We aren't."

Carly worried her bottom lip, imagining the mess she'd left back at the church. If she could trust Prissy, she'd call her, but since her best friend had taken it upon herself to avail herself of the groom's sexual charms, she wasn't the wisest choice for a confidante at this point in time.

Maybe she could start fresh somewhere, or at least wait until the uproar died down before returning home. After quickly reassuring herself that she was safer nowhere near Baton Rouge, at least for a while, Carly relaxed. One less thing to worry about and, hopefully, she would learn to be a better judge of people.

"We're headed west?" she asked, looking to the future, instead of the past.

Nodding, he kept his eyes on the late-afternoon traffic. "To Texas?"

He briefly took his attention off the road long enough to glance at her. "What makes you think so?"

"Your Texas drawl." When he glanced at her again, she felt more than saw his surprise. "It's not the same as a Louisiana accent," she quickly explained. "Or Georgia or Arkansas or Mississi—"

"Right." His long fingers flexed on the steering wheel. "I never realized I still had it," he muttered under his breath.

"That black hat's a good hint."

"Men wear Stetson's in Louisiana, too."

"But you're not from Louisiana."

This time his fingers gripped the steering wheel, and the hard, sharp angle of his jaw moved before he spoke. "Same thing as."

Carly wished he'd do more than glance at her. Having a conversation with someone she couldn't make eye contact with always made her uneasy. That's what had started her wondering about James over the past week. It wasn't that he never looked at her directly. He did, often. But lately there had been something in his eyes. Something that had begun to make her uncomfortable at times. He had never given her a reason not to trust him. In fact, he had swept her off her feet the first time she met him. She now understood what a whirlwind courtship was. Flowers, candlelit dinners, expensive trinkets and lots of attention. James certainly knew how to turn a girl's head. And he had been more than a gentleman with both her and her mama. But although she had made it to the age of twenty-six without making a major mistake with a man, she knew now that her judgment, of men especially, was practically nonexistent. She had always considered herself a good judge of character. Not that her family and close friends agreed. Now she had proof they were right.

"You always lived in Louisiana?"

So lost in thought, his question startled her, and she answered automatically. "Born and raised in Baton Rouge, like all the Albrights and Charpentiers. I guess we've been here forever. I'd even bet we were here before the city was founded." She turned to look at the man next to her. "What about you?"

"You're a betting woman?"

It was the third time he'd answered a question with a question, and she didn't like what it might mean. "No, what I meant was, where are you from?"

"Didn't we just cover that?"

It was exactly as she had suspected. He didn't want to answer her questions. What was he hiding? Was Prissy right? Was she too trusting? Well, she certainly had been where Prissy and James were concerned.

"Do you always do that?" she asked, hoping she wasn't as gullible as everyone told her she was.

"Do what?"

She gave a nervous little laugh. He wasn't making things look any better with his evasion. "Answer a question you don't want to answer with another question."

Once again the corner of his mouth turned up, and Carly wondered what a full smile looked like. Mercy goodness! She hadn't even had a good look at him when he'd helped her into the vehicle. *Pauvre Défunte Mamère*, rest her soul, had told her time and again that she would come to a bad end if she didn't curb her *impulsivité*. She had been in such a panic to get away from the church as fast and as far as possible, she hadn't given any thought to what kind of man he might be. Only that he had come along when she had needed someone the most. He could be anybody. A kidnapper, for instance. Although why anyone would want to do that, since she and her mother didn't have two nickels left to rub together, was beyond her. Things had been bad enough before the wedding, but after all the expenses, she wondered what would happen if she were held for ransom. Would he kill her? Or would he merely leave her in some horrid place to fend for herself?

"Should I be afraid of you?" she asked, suddenly praying that, if nothing else, this stranger was truthful.

"*Are* you?"

"See? You did it again. And that makes me wonder if I shouldn't demand that you stop this second and let me out." She had never done anything this reckless or foolish. But there hadn't been time to think through the situation. She'd needed a way out of the worst moment in her life, and he'd been there to save her. What would happen if she now needed rescuing from her rescuer?

Making certain he was watching the road and not her, she slowly reached for the doorhandle, grateful that her bouffant skirt hid her movement.

She froze when he leaned over to grasp the wrist of her free hand. He kept his eyes on the road and his voice low. "I wouldn't do that if I were you, sugar. Jumping from a car going ninety miles an hour isn't healthy."

Carly swallowed the lump of fear in her throat, acutely aware of the tingling in her fingertips from his touch.

Releasing her, he slowed the car as they entered heavier traffic. "I'm not going to hurt you."

"Yeah, right," she muttered under her breath.

His soft chuckle sent a warm shiver up her spine. "Trust me," he said, his voice setting butterflies free low in her middle. "The last thing I want is to see you hurt."

She ignored the flutterings and noticed that he was looking for a spot to pull off the road. If she could stall him long enough, make him think she was going along with this, maybe she'd get the chance to escape.

"Trust you?" she asked, hoping her voice wouldn't betray her nervousness. "I don't even know your name."

"What's yours?"

Frustration warred with fear and won. "Carolyn. Carolyn Albright. But my friends call me Carly."

"Nice to meet you, Carly. Mine's Dev Brannigan." Slowing almost to a stop, he pulled into the drive-through of a familiar hamburger chain. "You hungry?"

She started to tell him he couldn't change the subject. But when he turned in the seat to look at her, the words died on her lips.

One dark eyebrow arched over a sapphire-blue eye, the other was covered with a black leather patch, giving him a rakish appearance. Like a pirate.

Or the Devil.

While his traveling companion slept, Dev thought about her reaction to what must have been her first view of his eyepatch. Surprise had been the first emotion to cross her face. But it hadn't lasted more than a second. He hadn't seen the next thing coming, but he should have. If she had screamed, he would have been prepared. Not Carly Albright. Nope. She'd just matter-of-factly asked him if Dev was short for Devil.

Chuckling softly so he wouldn't wake her, he shook his head. Just like his mother, who had often told him she had named him for Lucifer, not a French ancestor. Carly certainly was straightforward. No keeping her hand close to her vest. And the questions! Right and left. He felt like a novice tennis player trying to field McEnroe's volleys. He had wanted to ease the fear she had eventually shown of him, but the less she knew, the better. At least for now. And until he could discover what, if anything, besides J.R.'s last-minute infidelity, had caused her to run out on her wedding, he wasn't revealing anything about himself until and unless it was absolutely necessary.

His older brother, Chace, referred to their former neighbor as a snake. Considering the story of how Chace had met his wife, Ellie, Dev agreed that the term fit. He preferred weasel. Like the predatory animal that sneaked into henhouses in the dark of night, J.R. did his damage and was gone before anyone was the wiser. Was Carly Albright his latest victim? Had she, like Ellie almost had, fallen for one of his schemes?

When he had helped her from the church, Dev's only thought had been to question her while he took her wherever she wanted to go. He hadn't planned anything more, until he learned she had nowhere to go. Now that she was in his care for however long, he hoped J.R. would come after her.

He had waited for the right moment to ask a few questions, but once they'd eaten and driven another thirty minutes, her eyelids had fluttered shut, hiding her blue-green eyes, and he hadn't wanted to disturb her. Especially when he noticed the dark circles under her eyes.

This wasn't the way he'd expected to be driving home, with an almost-bride on the run, but it sure beat the alternative. He was pretty certain J.R. hadn't recognized him, but even that didn't matter. No one, not even his family, had any idea what he did or where he lived. He had planned it that way. Maybe he would soon be able to tell them about his life. Then again, once they knew everything, they might not give a damn.

The miles ticked by while he considered how to let J.R. know where to find the blushing bride. By the time the sun blazed its lowering path to the horizon, and the highway led him into the heart of Shreveport, he had planned his next play.

When he pulled into the private parking area behind his building, he noticed one particular car and was glad to see it. He'd be able to play his first card without delay.

Turning off the engine, he looked at the woman next to him. He hated to wake her. Whether she exhibited outward signs of emotional exhaustion or not, he sensed she was pretty well drained. It wouldn't be anything at all to carry her to the elevator. She couldn't weigh that much, and he kept himself in good physical condition. People who knew him might think he had a cushy job, but he knew better. Not only did he have to be mentally alert at all times, but he sometimes needed the brawn to go with the brains. The patch over his eye was proof of that.

As he suspected, she didn't weigh more than some of the oil equipment he'd lifted when he'd worked with the drilling company. Carrying her to the elevator and from there into his private quarters, he took her straight to his bedroom. He would be too busy most of the night to need the bed himself and could always get a few winks on the sofa in the sitting room.

She didn't even stir when he gently placed her on top of the silk spread. Looking down at her in the soft glow of the small bedside lamp, he hoped the luck of meeting her when he did was good and not bad. His daddy had always told him he possessed the Devil's luck, but the sight of Carly, so peaceful and beautiful, made him wonder if he wasn't about to find out exactly what that meant.

Concerned that she might soon be uncomfortable, Dev wasn't sure what to do. She was obviously sleeping soundly. She might look like an angel in that wedding dress, but it wasn't something someone would want to sleep in. Should he try to get her out of it? There was no doubt she needed the sleep, and he probably could do it without waking her, but— But nothing. Hell, he wasn't about to try to strip her out of that thing. He wasn't crazy. The odds were against him that he could do it without giving a thought to what lay beneath the layers of lace and satin.

After finding an extra blanket, he covered her and searched for something she could wear when she'd had enough sleep. Knowing he probably wouldn't be there when she did awaken, he left her a note.

In the elevator he mentally went over his plan again. When it came to a stop, he walked down the hall to the security office, ready to put things into action.

"Greg," he said, after stepping into the room, "I need to get some information out as fast as possible."

His chief of security looked up from the bank of closed-circuit televisions stationed along one wall and shoved his glasses back up on his nose. "Out to the other casinos?"

Dev nodded. "Let's start with the ones here in Shreveport and see if that does the trick."

Without blinking an eye, Greg Tremain picked up a phone. "What do they need to know?"

Smiling at the man's efficiency, Dev took a seat next to him. "I expect Staton to be arriving in town within the next few days. Get word to him that the woman who left him standing at the altar is here at the Devil's Den."

The only indication that Greg knew things hadn't gone as planned was a nearly imperceptible raising of one eyebrow as he punched a number on the auto-dialer.

While Greg relayed the message to twenty-some Shreveport area casinos, Dev closed his eyes, imagining J.R.'s reaction to the news. He suspected that once J.R. learned where Carly was, he'd come after her. In the meantime Dev would get the full story of their relationship from Carly. If there was more to it than money—and he doubted it was love on J.R.'s part—he would soon know.

Greg waited, the phone to his ear, and turned to him. "Things didn't work out like you'd hoped?"

"Nope. But I have it covered," Dev said, thinking of Carly. "One more thing. As soon as Staton steps a foot through the door of this place, I want to know it."

"I'll alert the staff and make sure Security keeps their eyes open."

Standing, Dev put his hand on Greg's shoulder. "Thanks. I'll fill you in on everything as soon as I know myself."

He let himself out of the room while his most trusted employee followed his orders. Rotating his shoulders to ease the kinks from the long drive, he smiled. The pot was at the highest it had ever been, and the ante would soon go up. Once he had J.R. taken care of, he could return to the Triple B Ranch to face his brothers. He had a confession to make, and he didn't know how his brothers would react. He didn't expect it to be good. But until he could prove his worth as a member of the family by putting a stop to J.R. and the four-generation feud, he would have to wait. He could do that. With his ace sleeping soundly upstairs in his bed, he was certain he held the winning hand.

Chapter Two

Carly scratched at her neck, not yet awake but not asleep. Her fingertips recognized an unfamiliar texture, and she drowsily wondered what it was. Her flannel gown wasn't this itchy. As her mind slowly floated out of the dreamy state, she remembered it was April, and she didn't wear a flannel nightie in the spring. So why was there lace at her throat?

Her hand froze. *Of course*. She was in her wedding gown, an expensive creation of imported lace, seed pearls and creamy satin that her mother had insisted Carly must have, even though they couldn't afford it.

The cobwebs in her mind slowly receded, and she realized she wasn't at her wedding and she wasn't on her honeymoon. She scrunched her eyes tight and groaned. Had she really announced that she couldn't marry James?

Her mind whirled with images and sounds, of

Prissy's pale face and her mother's tear-filled eyes and anguished cry. Oh, yes, she'd done it. And now she would have to deal with it. That's what she got for not heeding *pauvre défunte Mamère's* warnings.

Memories flew at her like a whirlwind, settling finally on a devilishly handsome stranger. One whose very presence had been threatening and frightening, yet protective and calming. And he had certainly made her heart race, especially when he touched her. He'd come to her rescue, and they'd driven off in his Jeep. Yes, that's what she remembered. They'd gotten burgers and driven on, and she'd been so tired, so exhausted, that she must have fallen asleep.

But where was she now? Whose bed was she sleeping in? Like Goldilocks awakening when the three bears returned, she was afraid to open her eyes. She giggled nervously, wondering whether, if she did peek, she would see huge bears peering at her.

Feeling more than silly, she slowly opened her eyes. *See? No bears, you goose.* She let out a shaky sigh of relief. The room was empty. Of bears anyway and, thankfully, of people too.

Slivers of sunshine in the dusky room slipped through a slit in the drapes across from the bed. Moving carefully, Carly pushed back the blanket covering her and cautiously walked on silk-stockinged feet from the bed to the window. Her fingers trembled as she peeled the edge of the curtain aside a few inches. Bright light hit her full in the face, and she blinked, but she was determined to find out where she was. After she became accustomed to the brightness, she gazed out and then took a quick step back, the fabric slipping from her fingers. She spun around, taking in the room's furnishings and the personal pictures on the wall. This wasn't a motel room. This was…an apartment? And merely the bedroom.

On a large, upholstered club chair, she spotted her veil, draped across the back and trailing to the floor. She crossed the few steps to it and noticed a piece of paper atop a pile of what looked like clothing. Picking up the note, she squinted in the dim light and quickly read it.

Since you didn't bring luggage, you can wear these until we get you something more appropriate. When you're ready, give me a call and we'll have some breakfast.

It was signed "Dev," with a phone number under the name.

Carly moved the clothes aside and sank onto the chair, pressing the heels of her hands to her eyes. Mercy goodness, what had she gotten herself into? She'd bolted from the church without a thought as to what she was doing or what would happen to her. She hadn't even grabbed a bag. But then, her luggage had been tucked away in James's car so she wouldn't have bothered if she had even thought of it. Her wardrobe was the last thing on her mind when she'd burst through the church doors and the stranger had taken her away. She'd spent a sleepless night before her wedding wondering what to do, planning exactly what she'd say and when she'd say it, and praying she could go through with it. She certainly hadn't planned well.

Then again, when it came to her personal life, she never did. Between being too impulsive and her poor judgment, she had really botched things.

All she could do now was make the best of the situation she'd managed to get herself into. As bad as it might be, it couldn't be as bad as if she had gone ahead with the wedding.

Picking up the items she'd shoved aside, she held up one of the two and eyed it. A sweatshirt. The other piece of clothing was matching sweatpants, and both were several sizes too big. Since she didn't have a choice—it was her wedding gown or the sweatsuit or nothing—she stood and began to struggle out of her dress. Cursing each tiny satin-covered button in the back, she finally gave up and tugged at the fabric until she heard a rip, and the fasteners popped like popcorn around her.

Once freed, she ignored the wave of guilt caused by the damage she had done and shoved the cumbersome dress to her feet. Stepping out of it, she removed her nylons and shivered, then grabbed the clothing Dev had left and quickly put it on. The legs of the pants were a good ten inches too long, and she was forced to roll the waistband over and the hems up, so she could take a step without tripping. Shoving the sleeves up as far as possible, she looked around for a mirror. Seeing none above the massive dresser along one wall, she tried a door and found a bathroom.

One look in the mirror was enough to know it was a wonder her savior hadn't dumped her along the road. Mascara smudged beneath both eyes, and her hair looked as if it had been brushed with an egg beater. A drop of water on her finger removed the black marks, and a finger-combing tamed her hair to almost present-able.

Satisfied she could do nothing more with her ap-pearance, she passed through the doorway and spied a cordless phone on the table next to the bed. She grabbed it and the note, and quickly punched in the number Dev had left her.

"Brannigan," he drawled.

The man's voice was absolutely lethal. The sound of it warmed the blood running through her veins, and she closed her eyes. She could listen to it forever.

"Carly?"

She opened her eyes and sighed softly. "Thanks for the loan of the clothes."

He let out a whoosh of breath. "Sure. No problem. You okay?"

Was she? She really couldn't tell, still feeling a little shell-shocked and confused. "I think so."

"Good. What do you like for breakfast?"

"Breakfast?" She rarely ate in the morning and had often been chided by her mother for it. "Doesn't matter. Look, uh, Dev—"

"Stay put," he said, before she could finish. "I'll have something there in fifteen minutes."

"You don't need to do that. What I wanted to ask you is—"

But he'd hung up.

Fifteen minutes for breakfast? Was there a fast-food place nearby? A shop with coffee cake? Whatever, she didn't care, as long as he had the answers she needed and would be kind enough to help her. She was certain he hadn't saved her only to refuse to help her now. Even with the eye patch he wore, he looked reasonable.

Too antsy to be still, she decided to explore, hoping to discover where she was. That's all she needed to know, and if only he hadn't ended the call in such a rush, she would have asked. Once she had her bearings, maybe she could start making plans.

She opened a pair of double doors near the dresser and discovered a walk-in closet filled with shirts and suits, all neatly hung in double rows. The other set of doors led into an impressive living room. A corner fireplace dominated the room, along with an enormous window that spanned one wall. Walking behind a huge white leather sofa facing an entertainment center crowded with electronic equipment, she went to the window and stared out at the same view she'd had from the bedroom. She was several floors up and could see far into the distance, but it didn't reveal her location. All she could tell was that there was a city out there, with a slow-moving river running through it. She could be almost anywhere.

Wishing he would hurry so she could find out where she was, she took a seat on one of the matching white leather chairs that flanked the sofa. Knowing there was one thing she needed to do, she dialed the long-familiar number, hoping her host wouldn't mind a small long-distance charge.

"Mama?" she said, when her mother answered after two rings.

"Carly! Oh, honey, where are you? Are you all right? I'm absolutely appalled at what that James did to you. That awful man. Don't you worry, honey. He'll never be able to show his face again to anyone of any significance in Baton Rouge."

Carly waited until her mother took a breath, amazed at the difference between the anguished cry at the church and the comforting yet indignant concern her mother now conveyed. She smiled, knowing full well that her mother had sobbed to her closest friends, who had insisted that Carly had done the right thing, in light of what had happened. And what an enlightenment!

"I'm fine, Mama," Carly answered, when given the chance. "I just need some…I need some time away, that's all."

"Oh," her mother said, sounding a bit disappointed. "But I can understand. I don't know how you managed to do it, thinking I would be so very disappointed and knowing people would talk. And they have, Carly, I have to tell you. But they're talking about how utterly awful James was to do what he did to such a sweet girl like you."

But Carly knew that all the blame couldn't be laid at James's door. She had been the one taken in, the one who had judged him completely wrong. And if she had done that, there was no telling just how bad her judgment was. "I don't know when I'll be home, Mama," she said truthfully.

"Well," her mother said, dragging the word out, "I hope it's soon. We have to make new plans, now that you'll be living at home again."

Certain her mother had ditched the plan they'd made together, Carly hurried to answer. "You go right ahead and sell the house, Mama, and move into that new apartment. You'll like it so very much more than rambling in that big old house." And with the money from the sale, she knew her mother could pay off the debts and start fresh. They'd planned it down to the smallest detail.

"Don't worry about me," Carly said, fighting the tears that threatened. "I'm a big girl and can take care of myself."

But could she really? She had always been at home, and while many of her friends had married and settled down, she had taken over the responsibilities of running their large estate—an estate that had become a huge money pit.

"But, Carly—"

"No buts, Mama. It's time I strike out on my own. But I'll be in touch. I promise. Call Cousin Edward about the sale. And do it today, Mama, please."

"I just don't know…"

"You'll love that new apartment," she said, her heart aching. "I love you, Mama, and I'll talk to you again soon."

After her mother professed her own love, Carly hung up. She had spoken with her mother's cousin Edward at length about selling the house. He knew exactly what needed to be done, and he would watch over her mother until Carly returned. *If* she returned. But she couldn't now. Not yet. That was something she wasn't ready to face for a long time.

Dev didn't have any idea what Carly might like to eat, so he'd had the chef load up a cart with just about everything. His own breakfast had been hours ago, as was his habit. He didn't need to eat, and he slept only when exhaustion forced him to.

Unlocking the door to his private quarters, he pushed the cart into the room ahead of him. He immediately saw Carly perched on a chair, a frown marring her pretty features.

"Glad to see you made it through the night." He stopped next to the low table in front of her. "I hope you weren't too uncomfortable."

She gave him a small, shy smile. "I wouldn't know. Apparently, I slept through everything. I hope I wasn't a bother. If you'll just tell me—"

"Here," he said, passing her a plate to fill. "Dig in. I hope there's something you like."

Her eyes widened when he removed the shiny domed lids of several individual plates piled high with a variety of different foods. "I'm not a big breakfast eater," she began, her gaze on the offerings, "but this looks too good to pass up. Where did you get it? Is this a hotel?"

"Of sorts," he answered, handing her a cloth napkin.

She looked up to stare at him, surprise and a touch of fear evident in her eyes. He smiled and added two more fresh strawberries to her plate, then sat on the corner of the sofa near her. He wasn't quite ready to reveal her whereabouts. Until he could discover how much she knew about J.R., he'd keep the information to himself. When he was certain she wasn't involved in his stepbrother's nefarious activities, he'd answer her questions. The less personal ones, at least.

"Relax and enjoy your breakfast," he told her, crossing one foot over the other knee and leaning back to watch.

"Aren't you going to eat, too?"

"A little late in the day for breakfast for most people, don't you think?"

She placed her plate on the table in front of her, sighing, and looked up at him. "There you go again. A question for a question. I'm beginning to think you don't want to tell me anything. Am I right?"

"I'll answer your questions and maybe show you around when you're finished. How's that?"

Shrugging, she picked up her plate again and took a bite of fresh cantaloupe. While she was busy with her food, he studied her. As inquisitive as she was, he wondered how J.R. had managed to con her, if indeed he had. It was entirely possible that she was embroiled in the man's schemes. But she didn't strike Dev as the devious type.

He weighed the possibilities. Her angelic face and air of innocence might be an asset J.R. could put to good use. The man had fooled almost everyone with his false tales and easy-on-the-eyes appearance. But for a woman who'd left her intended at the altar, Dev wasn't ready to believe she wasn't involved in anything or even knew that the man she'd nearly married was nothing more than a thief.

"You don't seem too concerned for a bride who just jilted her groom," he pointed out.

The strawberry in her hand stopped at her open lips. She closed her mouth and returned the fruit to her plate, hanging her head, her shoulders drooping. When she looked up at him again, her eyes brimmed with tears and pink tinged her pale cheeks. If she was acting, she was one of the best he'd ever seen. But J.R. would find the best. Still, Dev had to quell the sympathy he suddenly felt for her.

"I made a…mistake," she said, ducking her head again.

"You mean you *had* to marry him?" His gaze slid down her body, wondering if she might be carrying the child of his sworn enemy.

"Mercy goodness! It isn't what you're thinking," she cried, her cheeks deepening to a rosy red. "We never… He didn't—"

"You aren't pregnant," he finished for her, ignoring his slight feeling of relief. "Then why was it a mistake?"

Pushing the plate of food away, she leaned back in the chair and closed her eyes. "This is very embarrassing," she said in a soft voice he had to strain to hear.

Had she been duped and was now too ashamed to admit she had been involved in anything that might be illegal? But he wasn't ready to trust her. Maybe she was playing on his sympathies, and he wasn't going to fall for it if she was. He wasn't sure what he could say to get her to open up to him, but he tried with, "You can tell me. I'm a good listener."

She shook her head, and a tear trickled slowly down her cheek.

"I promise not to judge you," he coaxed.

For a moment she didn't move, except to sink her teeth into her bottom lip and nod.

"He hurt you?" Dev asked when she didn't say anything.

"No, he never laid a hand on me. He was always a gentleman."

"I mean…emotionally," he tried.

She blew out a breath. "You mean because of Prissy."

"Prissy?"

"My maid of honor. Prissy is supposed to be my best friend."

"Then you *are* in love with him?" Somewhere deep inside, Dev almost hoped she would say she wasn't. And he didn't like thinking that. But if she wasn't, he didn't want to learn that this young woman was on the wrong side of the law.

Her chin lifted and her lower lip quivered. "I suppose it won't sound very good if I say I thought I was."

He smothered the slight stab of disappointment he felt. Yesterday, when he'd helped her leave the church, his only thought had been that she might give him some information about J.R. After all, the wedding wasn't going to take place, and he had lost his chance to corner the man. But because she felt she had nowhere to go, he didn't see any reason not to take advantage of the situation and use her to lure J.R. here on his own turf. It would be even better to confront him here. The bride might have taken offense to the groom being led away by police on their honeymoon. Especially now that he had met Carly.

But he found himself losing his perspective and wanting to help her out of whatever trouble she was in. Maybe he could still help her and nail J.R., too, but he'd have to have the full story before he could do it. And he had to keep his plans for the casino and J.R. uppermost in his mind. Getting sidetracked because of a pretty woman wasn't like him. He wasn't about to take that chance now, when he was so close.

"Tell me what the two of you were involved in."

She stared at him, her eyes wide. "Involved in? We were getting married. That's the only kind of involvement we had. And why were you at my wedding? Are you a friend of James? Or maybe family?"

Dev nearly laughed out loud. Family? *No*. Friend? Far from it. They had known each other since birth and had been enemies even before that. Four generations, to be exact. "I've known him a long time," he answered, unwilling to say more until he was sure that she wasn't involved in something unlawful.

And something in the "was" about loving J.R. still bothered him. "If you knew about his…uh, unfaithfulness before the wedding, why didn't you just call it off then?"

Placing her hands in her lap, she linked them tightly together and lowered her head. "I don't know. Janelle, one of my bridesmaids, phoned me the morning before to tell me the news. I was so confused and hadn't had much sleep. I didn't really know what to do until the last minute." She looked up at him and sighed. "There had been signs, but I ignored them."

"What signs?"

"Well, for one thing, he was impatient about the wedding date. He wanted to get married sooner than I had chosen. We finally convinced him that anything sooner would mean a shoddy wedding, and Mama wouldn't stand for that. Then he started acting strange as the wedding drew closer."

"In what way?"

"He…hovered, wanting to spend every second with me. He would get upset if we hit a snag in the wedding plans. He stopped caring about the wedding plans after a while, when he had been very involved in them in the beginning." She sighed, and her eyes filled with tears again. "I should've done something then. At least asked him what the problem was. But I excused it as pre-wedding jitters and continued with the wedding plans." She paused for a moment, looking down at her hands, still clenched in her lap. "But it's obvious there was something going on with Prissy, even then. Maybe he swept her off her feet like he had me. I don't know. And then there was Mama and Oak Hill Grove."

He shook his head, trying to make sense of it. "Oak Hill Grove is your home?"

She breathed a long sigh. "Yes. You see, it's been in the Charpentier family for years. It was passed down from my great-great-grandfather Charpentier to his son, to his son, and then to Mama when she married, because she has no brothers. But it's so old, and expenses and taxes have been so high and—" she lowered her head and shook it "—and Mama isn't very good with money. She went through what little bit Daddy left her, years ago."

Stunned, Dev stared at her. "You were marrying him for his money?"

He heard her sniff before she looked at him. "No, not at all. In fact, Mama and I made plans when we knew I would be getting married and moving into my own home. She would sell Oak Hill Grove, pay off the debts and move to a nice apartment."

Remembering what J.R. had done to others and nearly done to his oldest brother's wife before they married, Dev asked the only thing on his mind. "Was there oil on the land?"

"Oil? Why, no. We had it surveyed two years ago. Mama was hoping there might be. It would've been the answer to our prayers. But there isn't. Why do you ask?"

This was his chance to tell her how J.R. was no good, but he hesitated. "An answer to your difficulties maybe?"

"It would have been," she agreed with another sniff. "No one knows how bad things have become for us. Mama insisted that we always put up a good front. Even the cousins don't have any idea. Somehow, we've been able to fool everyone."

"And James didn't know this, either?"

"Oh, mercy, no! I never breathed a word to him. Why would I? There was no reason to. We had everything worked out. Our financial problems would be solved and still be our secret."

Dev got to his feet, turning to hide his smile. It would've served J.R. right if the wedding had occurred. In addition to his questionable real estate practices and other business ventures, the man owed a small fortune to enough casinos and money sharks across the country to keep him running for years. He was obviously hoping he could get his hands on the Albright's money and family name to hold off some of his debtors until he could find a way to pay them off, if not have enough money from the marriage to do it all. People were on to his oil schemes in Oklahoma and Texas. Probably Louisiana, too. Dev knew J.R. had tried his marriage scheme on at least one other unsuspecting woman. Carly didn't know how lucky she was that her prospective groom had committed his indiscretion.

That wasn't the problem now. Dev was convinced

J.R. still didn't know the truth and would come look-ing for Carly. But Dev couldn't keep her here against her will. If she stayed of her own free will—and he would see that it was—all he had to do was wait and play out the hand to the last card. Even if she moved on, J.R. would still come looking for her at the casino.

Carly pushed away from the table and stood to walk to the windows. "Would you tell me about James?" she asked, turning back to look at Dev. "You seem to know him well."

Dev wasn't sure if it would be better or worse for her to hear the truth. He didn't know her well enough to assess how much damage it could cause. But she deserved to know as much as he felt he could reveal.

"You're not the only woman he's conned," he ad-mitted. "My older brother's wife, Ellie, had a similar experience with him."

Carly's eyes widened. "Did she marry him?"

"No, it didn't come to that. But he had learned there was oil on land that she and her brothers owned. He was trying to buy it, and when he couldn't, because her brothers refused to sell, proposing marriage was his next step. As it turned out, Ellie didn't fall for it. But from what I know, it was a close call for her."

"Oh, my!" she whispered, her face pale.

Dev hurried to her side and reached out to steady her, afraid she was going to faint. "Are you okay?"

"Yes," she said, her voice breathless, "but I had no idea…" She looked up at him, adding a smile. "I can't thank you enough for telling me."

Fearing he might have caused more damage, he decided to change the subject, hoping that doing so, she might have time to come to terms with all that had happened. "What size do you wear?"

Surprised by his question, Carly forgot her own questions. When his one-eyed gaze roamed from the tips of her toes to the top of her head, she shivered. Mercy goodness! If he could make her feel that warm by looking at her with one eye, how hot would she get if he had two?

"Eight," she managed to answer. "Why?"

When he released her but didn't answer, she watched him cross the room and pick up the phone. He punched a number on the keypad and waited. "Janet, can you bring me up a size eight swimsuit? No, just pick a pretty one and have it sent up to my quarters. Thanks."

Carly wondered just who this man was who had come to her aid when she had needed it the most. "Are you going to tell me where we are?" she asked when he had finished the call.

"You're in Shreveport, sugar. And this is The Devil's Den, the biggest hotel and casino in the area."

"And we're in your…?" she asked.

"My suite."

"And I suppose you own this place?"

"All seventy-five-thousand square feet of it. How old are you?"

"I'm old enough to gamble, if that's what you're wondering."

Her warmth went up another notch when he smiled at her. "You won't mind not participating, will you?" he asked.

"I've never been in a casino, but—"

They were interrupted by the door buzzer, and he

went to answer it. He didn't open the door wide enough for her to see anything, but she heard him thank whoever it was, and then he turned to her with a beautiful aqua swimsuit on a hanger.

"There's a nice pool downstairs," he said, walking back to the table. "I thought you might enjoy a swim. While you're doing that, I'll find something else for you to wear. Anything more you need?"

The consequences of her actions the day before were quickly catching up with her. Now that he had told her about James, she was ashamed to admit that she didn't have a penny on her. She had somehow managed to lose even the one tucked in her shoe for good luck.

"What?" he asked. "You don't like to swim?"

She shook her head and then took a deep breath. "I can't pay you."

"So?"

"You've already been too kind to get me out of the scrape I was in. If it hadn't been for you, well, I don't know what would've happened at the church. As it is, I don't know how I'll repay you for your kindness, much less the swimsuit."

"Forget it," he said, with a wave of his hand. "We all get in a scrape from time to time."

"But if I had just one nice outfit, I could look for a job, and I could pay you back with my first check."

His mouth drew down in a frown. "Don't worry about a job right now. You've been through a lot. You're probably worn out. I hear planning a wedding can do that."

"Well, yes," she admitted. And so could planning how to dump the groom.

"We'll find a way to work it out."

"But I can't stay here."

His frown deepened. "Why not?"

"Why, because it...because I..." She stood and planted her hands on her hips, glaring at him. "Well, think about it. How would it look?"

He reached out, taking her hand, his smile slanted and his eye twinkling. "For you or for me?"

She had to force herself to swallow to kick-start her heart. "For either of us."

Holding her hand, he gently guided her toward the bedroom. "Believe me, sugar, there isn't much left of my reputation."

What was he thinking of? Surely she hadn't led him to think she was the kind of woman who would repay a man with sex. Mercy sakes! Hadn't she just made the mistake of her life with one man? Had she made an even worse one by trusting *this* man?

She pulled away. "But—"

"But nothing. I'll sleep on the sofa and you can have the bed."

"But—"

He stopped in the doorway, silencing her with a shake of his head and handed her the swimsuit. "Get changed. I'll meet you at the elevator on the ground floor and take you to the pool. As long as you stay out of the casino, you don't have to worry about your reputation."

"Oh. Okay." The sudden disappointment she felt surprised her. Mercy goodness, she couldn't have been hoping he had something else in mind.

As she walked into the bedroom, she heard him

leave the suite, and she breathed a sigh of relief. What had come over her? For the past few days she had hardly known herself. She had always been a good daughter, but when she learned James had slept with Prissy, her impulse had been to run, and she had grabbed the chance. She hadn't thought of her mama, only of herself. But even knowing deep in her heart how selfish that was, she simply couldn't be sorry.

She definitely needed some time to sort through things. Maybe time would improve her bad judgment, and she would learn to be more cautious.

But here she was, practically living with a strange man. Even worse, she couldn't take her eyes off him. What had come over her, indeed?

Chapter Three

"Mr. Brannigan?"

Dev looked up from his desk and smiled at his secretary. "Problems, Shirley?"

"Not for you," she said with a shake of her gray curls. "For me and the rest of us here, who knows?"

She handed him an envelope, and he glanced at the return address. Norbert Jenkins of Miami, Florida. This wasn't the first reply he'd received since getting word out that the Devil's Den was for sale. But the others had been corporations, and he didn't trust how they would treat the employees who stayed. That was the most important thing to him, as much as the amount of the bid. No matter who bought the place, he wouldn't take a penny less than what it was worth. And it was worth a gambler's fortune.

Grabbing a letter opener, he slit open the envelope and pulled out the neatly folded paper. He scanned it quickly, interested only in the offer. When he found it, his eyes widened. It was a fair and reasonable offer he could take with no qualms.

"I'll handle this later, Shirley," he said, filing the letter in a drawer. "Thanks for bringing it to my attention."

She nodded, but hesitated as if she had something more to say. He suspected he knew what it was, and to keep peace, he thought it wise to hear her out. Again.

"Is there something else?" Leaning back in his chair, he waited for the inevitable.

She nodded and took the chair across the desk from him. "You know, we really aren't excited to see the Den change ownership. Isn't there some way you could keep from selling it and still do whatever it is you have to do?"

He couldn't imagine going home to the Triple B Ranch while he still owned the casino. Not that his brothers would care what he'd been doing for the past fifteen years. But he had made up his mind long ago that if and when he returned home, he wouldn't take along any reminders of the years he'd spent away. He wanted a clean break if his brothers allowed him to stay. It was time he did more than send money and pay for legal services they didn't know about.

His younger brother, Trey, had gone against all odds and turned their childhood home into a dude ranch. Dev hadn't been crazy about the idea, and Chace, the oldest, had been dead set against it in the beginning. But by all reports, they were doing well.

"No one can run the Devil's Den like you can," Shirley said, breaking into his thoughts.

"I appreciate your loyalty, Shirley, and that's why I'm being particular about the buyer."

"He may not have a staff to work with, once you're gone."

"That's why I told all of you that I was considering the sale." Dev rubbed at his right eye, thinking of the handful of people who'd jumped ship at the news. He'd been afraid he'd lose more than half of his employees, but he hadn't counted on how loyal they'd been. Many of them, like Shirley and Greg, had become a surrogate family to him. But he wanted his real family, if they'd have him.

He stood and circled the desk, stopping in front of her. "I won't sell it to anyone who'd be a hard task-master. You know that."

"Yes, I do." She pulled a tissue from her pocket, sniffed as she dabbed at her eyes and rose to her feet. "It's just…well, it's like you're divorcing us or something."

Dev chuckled and guided her to the door. "I'll have to remember to demand visitation."

She patted his arm. "You be sure to do that. I'll hold you to it, you know."

"You have my promise."

Although her eyes still sparkled with unshed tears, she managed a smile and settled behind her own desk. "You'll let us know as soon as you make your decision on the buyer?"

"Cross my heart." He marked an *X* on his chest and then checked his watch. "Looks like it's time to make the rounds. I'll see you tomorrow. And, Shirley?" he added, placing his hands flat on her desk and leaning down to look at her.

"Yes?"

"Don't worry, okay?"

Waiting until she nodded, he left the offices and took the elevator to the ground floor, wondering how he'd been blessed with such a good staff of people. In the three years he'd owned the casino, there had only been one or two occasions when he'd had any trouble. And that was only because the casino had climbed to the top of the list as far as gamblers were concerned.

When the elevator doors slid open, he stepped out and surveyed the room before him with a smile on his face. Yeah, the Devil's Den was doing all right. He'd gone from a drifting oil worker to a successful casino owner in what seemed like the blink of an eye, but it had taken every cent that first year.

Strolling through the enormous room, he nodded at several dealers as he passed them, but came to a halt when he saw Carly standing near one of the blackjack tables, totally absorbed in the game.

Trying not to attract attention, he made his way over to her and clasped his hand around her bare upper arm. Tingles shot into his fingers and up his arm, and he nearly jerked his hand away. But he couldn't let her stand here in nothing but her swimsuit and a towel wrapped around her waist. Even if she had been fully dressed from chin to toes, he couldn't let her wander the casino.

"Go back up to the suite," he whispered in her ear, pulling her away from the table.

She glanced over her shoulder and looked up at him. "I never knew how interesting a casino was. Are most people here winners or losers?"

"It depends on the person and what he's playing."

"Or her?"

"Yes. But not you." He hustled her to the elevator and stepped inside, punching the button for the top floor. As it rose, he watched the numbers above the door light up, not certain that he should look at her. He hadn't missed the fact that she looked sexy as sin in the swimsuit. "Do me and yourself a big favor and stay out of the casino."

"It's so fascinating," she said, as if she hadn't heard him. "I've been watching, and I think I'm beginning to get the hang of some of it."

"You don't have any money, remember?"

"You could loan me some," she said sweetly. "And when I win, I can pay you back double your investment."

Gritting his teeth to check his groan, he grabbed her and turned her to face him. "Stay out of the casino," he managed to say.

She stared at him, her eyes wide and innocent, their blue-green depths urging him closer. Her pink tongue hesitantly slipped out to lick her lips, and he found himself wanting to nibble them to see if they were as soft and luscious as they looked.

"Why?" she whispered.

Before he lost control, he came to his senses and dropped his hands, turning away from the temptation. "Because I said so."

She was quiet, even after the doors opened and he followed her into the suite. Regretting his harsh tone, he offered her a soft drink from the small refrigerator hidden behind the leather bar. "I'm sorry, but you'll have to trust me on this, Carly."

She shrugged and avoided looking at him. "Like you said, I don't have any money to gamble, and since you aren't willing to loan me any, there isn't much else I can do."

"It's for your own good."

She gave an unladylike snort. "You sound like my mama. That's what she always says, too."

Not liking the comparison, he ignored her remark. "Is there anything special you'd like for dinner?"

She tilted her head and looked at him. "Do you always eat dinner this early?"

He crossed the room and opened the drapes. "Does it look early to you?"

Stepping up beside him, she gave a funny sigh that twisted something inside him. "That sunset is beautiful," she said turning to look up at him. "You're very lucky."

Dev couldn't stop looking at her. In the blazing glow of the sun dipping below the horizon, the soft features of her face were alight with wonder. He moved toward her, ready to take her in his arms and kiss the lips that were forming a small, wistful smile. But he caught himself and pulled back.

"Lobster," he said, remembering that he needed to order dinner. Maybe over a table of food he would be able to get himself together. He cleared his throat as if it would clear his mind. "Charles does a mean lobster. Would you like some? For dinner?" he asked as he moved across the room to the telephone, putting as much distance as possible between them.

"Lobster would be wonderful," she answered. As he punched in the room service number, she passed by him. "If there's time and it's okay, I think I'll take a shower and rinse the chlorine out of my hair."

The image of a lathered-up Carly, water streaming through her auburn hair and down her bare shoulders stopped him cold. He nodded, barely hearing the voice on the other end of the line. "What?" he said into the phone as Carly disappeared into the bedroom.

"Room service," Patti repeated. "What would you like, Mr. Brannigan?"

Poor Patti would blush if she had any idea of what he would really like. And Carly would probably slap him. "The lobster dinner for two, Patti," he answered. "And send a bottle of wine from my special stock to go with it." He would wine and dine Carly. But he wouldn't touch her, no matter how much he wanted to. There was no sense letting things get out of hand. He had more control than to let that happen. But it was pretty clear that Carly stretched that control to the limit.

Carly had just finished combing the damp tangles from her shoulder-length hair when there was a knock at the bathroom door.

"Dinner is here," Dev said from the other side.

Placing the complimentary hotel comb he had given her on the counter, she checked her reflection in the mirror. She could use a little makeup, but she wasn't about to ask Dev to put out any more money on her. She owed him too much as it was. Just how would she repay him? He obviously wasn't going to help her win any by loaning her some gambling money.

Shaking the worry from her mind, she opened the door and walked through the bedroom into the sitting room. The small table in the far corner was covered with a snowy cloth and set for two. Dev stood beside it, holding two candles in candleholders, a perplexed expression on his face. Her first thought was of J.R.'s candlelit dinners, but it was plain to see that Dev wasn't a pro at them. Still, she planned to be cautious.

"Allow me," she said and crossed the room to take the candles from him. "At least I can do something."

"Thanks." He handed them to her with a wry smile and a twinkle in his eye. "Now you know my secret. I never learned how to set a table."

"Setting a proper table and writing thank-you notes are my specialty," she told him as she placed the candles on the table. "Thanks to *pauvre défunte Mamère*."

He pulled out a chair and waited while she finished with the candles and took the seat he offered. "Your grandmother, right? I'm not as familiar with French as I probably should be."

"Yes," she said, sighing as he took the chair across from her. "My mother's mother. And I miss her dreadfully. Most of the time."

The cork on a bottle of wine slipped out. "Most of the time?"

She watched him pour the golden liquid into the glasses and nodded. "She was wonderful, but sometimes not so…kind, so *aimable*. There were times when she expected more than someone could give, and she could find anyone's smallest fault."

"She expected perfection?"

"Exactly," Carly said, smiling because he understood so perfectly. "I think I would've been a disappointment to her if she hadn't loved me. But although she never failed to correct my slightest mistake, she never did it without letting me know that she did it from the heart."

"My father was like that. A perfectionist. Had all our lives planned out. I always thought he was just a manipulative, domineering man. But looking back, he did it because he wanted us to succeed and be proud of our successes."

She detected a note of sadness in his voice. "Yes. *Pour votre propre bien*. For your own good," she said, translating with a smile. "I can't count the number of times she said that. And Mama, too." Studying the plate of food in front of her, she hated the thought of admitting her faults, but she couldn't stop. "And they were often right. But not always," she said, glancing up at him.

His eyebrow went up as he looked at her. "Like your wedding?"

She grinned at him. "You're quick."

"One of *my* specialties," he replied with his own grin.

Easy conversation weaved through their enjoyment of the dinner, pleasing Carly with its touch of camaraderie. There were so many things she wanted to know about him. And she didn't forget the note of sadness she had heard.

"When did you lose your father?" she asked, hoping he wouldn't think she was prying.

For a moment he was silent. "Not long after I graduated from high school. He died of a heart attack."

Carly was disappointed that in that silent moment, he had pulled a mask, hiding his feelings from her. But she couldn't blame him. He didn't know her, and although she had poured out a part of her heart to him at breakfast and now at dinner, too, she knew he would never do the same. After all, he was a man. She wasn't too naive to know that they often kept their feelings guarded.

"I'm sorry." Wiping the butter from her fingers onto her napkin, she leaned back to study him. "You said 'us' earlier. How many of you are there?"

"My two brothers and me," he answered without hesitation. "I lost my mother when I was five, so it was only the guys. Hence my poor knowledge of table setting," he added with a grin. "What about you?"

"Only me," she said, sighing. "Which is why Mama relies so much on me. She's been widowed for twelve years, and although she's still a lovely woman, I doubt she'll ever marry again."

"She was devoted to your father?"

"Oh, yes, even in spite of his gambling."

"Oh. I'm sorry."

She had to laugh at the look on his face. "Don't be sorry. He was a wonderful man. He just had that one problem. Unfortunately, he managed to go through a sizable family fortune over the course of several years. And Mama has no head for money at all."

"But you do?"

"When I have some," she said, with a sad smile. "At least I've been able to keep Oak Hill Grove, in spite of taxes and the cost of repairs. But money only goes so far," she added, shrugging, "and a name doesn't produce cash."

"A name can be an advantage."

"Or a disadvantage."

He cocked his head to the side and looked at her. "How so?"

She took a deep breath and blew it out. "Look at me. No skills. How am I to find employment? The South— at least my South—has·done a disservice to the young women from its older, wealthy families."

"It can't be that bad, Carly."

"No?" She shook her head. "I wish you were right. But I was raised in a different world from yours. A feminine world, where women of wealth don't lift a finger or even have thoughts of their own. We move within our own circle of friends. Parties, picnics, soirees, even a tea or two thrown in, just for the fun of it, of course. Why, I'm surprised we didn't use calling cards!"

"I actually like that old-fashioned practice. No surprises."

She couldn't stop her smirk. If only he would take her seriously. "If I wasn't a lady, I'd snort at that comment." She nearly laughed out loud when his eyebrow arched in comic disbelief. "We had servants. Or at least Mama and I did until we had to let them go because we couldn't afford the luxury anymore."

"You can cook?"

"No, we kept Cook. She'd been with us too long to leave." When he laughed at that, she wasn't sure whether to leave the room or laugh with him. "It isn't funny."

He sobered immediately. "No, you're right, it isn't. But I'm sure you have some talent, if only as a social secretary or something."

"My name isn't going to open doors." But she had talked enough about herself. And she shouldn't be so trusting. Just because he had told her about James—if it was the truth—how did she know that the man in front of her wasn't just as bad?

"What about yours? Is your name an advantage for you?" she asked, curious to know more.

"Not here. I'm only a corporation. But back home, the answer would be yes."

She thought about that. "So if I ever go to…Texas? Will the name Brannigan be my ticket?"

"Still fishing?" he asked with a wicked smile. "If I were you, I wouldn't use that name to gain admittance to genteel society. We're a rough-and-tough bunch."

Without thinking, she asked the question she had wanted to ask since she had first seen him. "Did rough-and-tough earn you the patch?"

Tilting his head to one side, he looked at her, but said nothing.

She bit her lip, worried that she had offended him. "I'm sorry. I shouldn't have asked. I'm just…curious."

"No, it's all right," he finally said. "In fact, most people are dying to ask but don't. It frightens some. I don't know why. And there's nothing romantic about it or how it happened, either. We had a bit of a problem with a guest who had had too much to drink. In the process of showing him the exit, my cornea was scratched. The patch is temporary and will be a thing of the past in another three weeks or so."

"Too bad," she said with a shake of her head and a smile. "I have to admit, it does give you a certain rakish look."

Dev laughed and stood, moving around the table to offer her his hand. "I've noticed that your perception is shared by others. If you're finished, I'll have someone clear."

Placing her hand in his, she was shocked at the heat

radiating from her fingers to the pit of her stomach. "I don't mind cleaning up."

"No. That's what the staff is for." She frowned and started to argue, but he continued. "They're well paid, Carly. They'd be offended if you did their job. You should know that."

"Yes, you're right," she answered, feeling contrite.

"I have business to attend to," he explained as he led her to the sofa. "I probably won't be back for hours. Enjoy my movie collection or whatever you'd like to do. Just don't go near the casino."

Nodding, she settled on the sofa, wishing she could go with him. Curiosity was getting the best of her, and she was dying to see how the business was run. Not to mention giving the roulette wheel a spin or two, or playing a few hands of blackjack. After all, her father's blood ran through her veins. But Dev had been nothing if not clear about the gambling, which was probably a blessing. She didn't have the right to flaunt his request.

"I'll probably go to bed soon," she told him, hiding a sudden yawn with the back of her hand. "I guess I'm not slept out yet."

"Take the bed. The sofa works fine for me."

Reaching out, he touched her cheek with his hand. "Sleep well, then."

At the door, he turned to look at her before he stepped out. "If you need anything, call room service. It's available twenty-four hours. And if you need me, call my cell phone. I'm only a number away."

"Thank you."

"Good night, Carly," he said before closing the door behind him.

"Good night, Dev," she whispered, but he was gone. A good thing, too, she decided. He was far too attractive for her own good. And she reminded herself that she couldn't yet trust her judgment.

"Thanks for taking care of it, Greg," Dev told his chief of security. Closing the security office door behind him as he left the room, he stifled a yawn and thought of Carly. He hadn't had time to check on her since they'd shared dinner the night before. Even though he had tried to grab a few winks on the sofa, the night had been too busy with small emergencies to afford him much rest.

There had been no sign of J.R., but the gambling would call to him. By the time he arrived in Shreveport, the word would be out about Carly's whereabouts. On Dev's orders, Greg had contacted the authorities, who were almost as eager as Dev was to get their hands on the weasel. He could taste the sweet revenge of having J.R. behind bars.

Making a last walk-through of the casino, Dev wasn't surprised that the place was relatively quiet. It was late morning and only a few people stood or sat around the gaming tables. He greeted one of the regulars with a smile, but it died on his lips and he came to a stop when he saw Carly standing at the roulette table.

Damn her! As a quick precautionary measure in case J.R. had slipped past security, he scanned the room as he strode to her side, hoping he could control his anger.

"May I see your identification, ma'am?" he said softly in her ear.

Her head whipped around to reveal deep fear in her eyes, but that quickly changed to recognition and relief. "Oh, Dev, it's you."

So angry he could barely speak, he wrapped his fingers around her upper arm. "How dare you defy me."

"B-but…" she stammered as he not so gently wove a path through the tables to the elevator. "I was only passing through. And I hadn't been there for more than a couple of minutes."

"And I told you not to go near the casino," he growled as they stepped into the elevator. He knew that even a half minute could be dangerous to a gambling addict. She might not be one, but she easily could be.

Stabbing the button for the penthouse floor with his finger, he gritted his teeth to keep from lashing out at her. If J.R. were to see her before Dev or security could get to him, he might be able to con Carly again. For her sake, Dev couldn't let that happen.

"You can let go of me now," Carly said, her voice soft and repentant. "I won't be going anywhere."

Dev silently watched the elevator's progression upward and was thankful it was fast. If it had been slower, he may have yelled at her. In public.

He had to choke back a chuckle at the thought, but he managed to hang on to his frown. Better to let her think he was still mad. Better for both of them.

With a soft *whoosh* the doors opened, and he followed her to his suite. Reaching around her to unlock the door, he was careful not to get too close. If he didn't watch himself, there was no telling what might happen.

But just as he was ready to open the door, she turned

to look up at him. "I'm sorry, Dev. I shouldn't have been in the casino."

The pure contrition in her eyes nearly buckled his knees. "Inside," he growled, throwing the door open. This time he was angry at himself for letting her get to him. He quickly reminded himself that she had disobeyed his orders. "Sit down," he ordered when they were both inside the room.

She walked to the sofa, her head lowered, and started to do as he said, but she stopped. "I prefer to stand, if you don't mind."

For a moment he was speechless. He couldn't help but admire her for her spunk. Most people shied away from him and immediately asked how high when he told them to jump. But not Carly. No, sir. She was determined to hold her ground and stand up for herself. It was amazing, especially after what she had been through.

"Whatever you like," he managed to reply.

"Why won't you let me go into the casino?" she asked before he could say more.

"Why do you need to?"

"Because it's fascinating. Is there something wrong with watching? Do you lose money on people who watch?"

"No. Gamblers lose enough money to compensate for those who don't play."

"So there's no harm to you or the casino if I simply watch, right?"

"Casinos can be rough places," he said, avoiding what he would have to tell her about J.R. "Fights are known to break out at the slightest provocation. Innocent bystanders have been hurt. Take a look at what can happen." He leaned closer, until they were almost nose to nose. "Is that enough reason?" When her eyes widened, he stepped back. "By the way, that dress is very becoming on you."

She blinked at him once, then looked down and smoothed her hand over the skirt of the dress he had left for her while she slept. "It's lovely, Dev, but you shouldn't have."

Her gaze locked with his, and the view of her sweet face caused him to forget how angry she had made him. Somehow he needed to find a way to restore it. "I can't imagine what people would have thought if they'd seen you wandering around in my old sweatsuit, that's all."

"I'd like to repay you for everything, and I think I'd really be good at blackjack, so if you'd loan—"

"Stop it!" He shook his head. She was making him crazy. Forget needing an incentive for anger. Carly managed to try his patience beyond sainthood. He softened his tone, but not his heart. "You cannot go into the casino, and that's all there is to it."

"*Pour mon propre bien?*" she asked, the sarcasm in her voice clear.

"Yes. For your own good, Carly. For your *safety*."

Her eyes narrowed as she stared at him. "It's more than a fight breaking out, isn't it?"

As he let out a long breath, the tension that had built inside eased. It was time to tell her as much of the truth as he could. He knew now that she wasn't part of J.R.'s schemes, only an innocent who had fallen for one of them.

"Yes. It is. I expect J.R., James, will come looking

for you. He saw you leave the church with me. He's a wanted man, Carly. White-collar crimes, so nothing for you to be worried about. He'd rather run and hide than fight. Or inflict harm," he added, seeing her frightened expression. "I've instructed Security to call me as soon as he steps in the door."

"Then there shouldn't be a problem," she said. But he could still see hesitation in her eyes.

"He could slip past them. And if he found you…"

"I can't believe he would hurt me."

"No, neither do I. Not physically. But he's a professional con man. He might find a way to talk you into leaving with him. Knowing you, you'd tell him about your money woes in the middle of nowhere. Then he would ditch you. Do you like walking? Long distances?"

She shook her head and looked away. When she looked back at him, he could tell she hadn't needed time to give his words a lot of thought. "To be honest, I'd rather not see him again. Ever."

"Then that settles it," he said with a quick nod. "No casino."

She took a step closer. "What if you were to stay with me while I played?"

"Someone might think we were cheating."

Her eyes twinkled and widened in mock horror. "In your own establishment?"

He knew she wasn't a seductress, but seduction oozed from her. He was tempted. So very tempted. But he fought it until he had himself under control. "People will think just about anything."

"What about some of your security people? The ones not in uniform. I've seen them wandering the room with a look of fake interest on their faces. One or two of them could stay close by, and if anything happened…"

Before he knew what he was doing, he had pulled her next to him. His lips were on hers, crushing at first, but softening when she moved to wind her arms around his neck. Her body pressed against his, and he felt her heat. The soft angles of her body seemed to melt into him. When he teased her lips with his tongue, she opened immediately, and he groaned with pleasure. Ironically it was her response that brought him to his senses and the kiss to a halt.

"I'm sorry," he said, releasing her and raking a hand through his hair. "I shouldn't have done that, and I apologize. I took advantage, and I've always been a gentleman."

It was clear that she was stunned, but whether it was by the kiss they had shared or because he had ended it abruptly, he couldn't tell.

She turned away, but before she could take a step, he reached for her hand and stopped her. She turned back to look at him but wouldn't meet his gaze. "It's all right," she said.

Taking a deep breath, he let it out slowly, wondering what he could do to atone for yet another sin. "I have a deal to offer you," he said, letting go of her hand. "I'll give you the run of the hotel—anywhere you want to go—in exchange for your promise not to go near the casino. Unless you'd rather I take you home."

Disappointment flashed in her eyes when she looked at him, but she offered him a smile. "No. Not home. So I guess it's better than nothing."

He held out his hand in a gesture of agreement. "Deal?"

She took it without hesitation. "Deal."

They stood for a moment, their gazes locked, and Dev felt the awkwardness the kiss caused pass. It had to, and the force that had driven him to do it had to be stopped. They were like night and day. Oil and water. She was the eternal optimist, while he had always been cautious and suspicious. She was impulsive, while he led his life on a planned schedule. She trusted people, while he trusted only the people closest to him.

But most of all, he had no future, and he wouldn't take advantage of her any more than he already had.

Chapter Four

Shaken by Dev's kiss, Carly waited until he left the suite before sinking to the nearest chair. Letting out a long, wishful sigh, she was grateful that he had stopped the kiss when he had. Her knees still felt like the muscles had completely vanished. Never in her entire life had she felt this way. Oh, she'd shared kisses with boys she knew when she was younger, and of course with men as she grew older. But even James's kisses hadn't made her feel the way Dev's did. She was in trouble. Big trouble.

Although she wasn't crazy about agreeing to his deal, she guessed that he was probably right. She had no business in the casino, no matter how curious she might be and how much it drew her. After all, her father had gambled away a sizable family fortune, leaving the family pinching pennies.

But it wasn't money problems that crept into her

mind. It was the feel of Dev's lips on hers. His strong arms pulling her closer until she could feel the beat of his heart, while her own heartbeat raced, faster and—

She shook her head and took a deep breath. No more of *that*. She was a bigger fool than she had thought if she hadn't learned a lesson from her father's gambling. And Dev was a gambler, too. How could he not be, as the owner of his own casino?

What she *should* be thinking about was what she would do if James came to the casino looking for her. She wasn't exactly sure how he would learn where she was, but considering what Dev had told her about her former fiancé—if Dev was telling the truth—he would have ways of finding out the information.

She was interrupted by the waiter, who had come to collect their dinner things and put aside her worries. Dev had given her the run of the hotel, and she was going to make good use of it. Maybe if she could learn enough, she might be able to talk Dev into giving her a job.

"Where do you take those?" she asked the waiter as she followed him out of the suite.

As the nice-looking young man continued down the hallway with the cart, he looked at her over his shoulder. "Why?" he asked, his eyebrows drawn together over the bridge of his nose.

Carly shrugged. "Just wondering." She followed him to the service elevator, hidden behind a door near the ice and soft-drink machines. "Mr. Brannigan said I could go anywhere in the hotel that I wanted to," she said at his look of surprise when she followed him into the elevator. She decided not to add that she wasn't allowed in the casino. No sense making herself look bad.

"The boss said that?"

He looked skeptical, and Carly rushed on. "Oh, yes. So, you see, it's all right with him if I follow you. Really."

The waiter's wary looked changed to one of unconcern. "Whatever you want to do, I guess." He moved the cart to one side and punched a button on the panel.

"Do you like him?" Carly asked, as the elevator moved downward.

"Mr. Brannigan?" he asked. When she nodded, he answered, "Yeah, he's an okay guy. He makes us toe the line. No goofing off. Well, not that he's aware of," he added with a secretive grin. "And the pay's good."

"Then you like working here for him."

"You bet."

The elevator doors slid open before Carly could ask anything else, and she followed the waiter through a maze of hallways. They finally came to a stop at a pair of metal swinging doors.

The waiter turned to look at her. "You sure it's okay if you come in here?"

"Of course it is," she assured him. "I wouldn't do anything to get you or anyone else in trouble. You can even ask him, if you think you should."

He hesitated for a moment. "Nah," he said. Pushing the cart through the doors, he motioned for her to follow him. "Just stay out of the way," he cautioned.

Carly was amazed. The room was bustling with activity as dishes were being prepared and carts were being brought back from meals already finished in guests' rooms. The room was dreadfully hot and horribly noisy, but she found it fascinating.

Touching the waiter on the arm, she asked, "Would you mind telling me your name?"

"It's David."

She stuck out her hand. "Hi, David. I'm Carly."

He took it and gave it a quick shake. "Nice to meet you, Carly," he said with a smile. "But I'd better get busy. Don't want anybody to think I'm goofing off."

She watched him push the cart into a far corner of the room, where other carts were being unloaded. Remembering that she needed to stay out of the way, she searched for a spot in the room where she could see everything, yet not be a bother. Finding it, she quickly became accustomed to the noise and watched the activity in the room.

She didn't know how long she had been standing there when someone touched her shoulder. Afraid she was in someone's path, she moved away, but a gentle hand pulled her back again, and she looked up to see Dev.

"Having fun?" he asked.

"It's fascinating," she told him, ignoring the fluttering in her stomach.

He laughed and smiled at her. "You find pretty much everything fascinating, don't you?"

"I suppose I do," she answered with her own smile. "This may all be old hat to you, but it's all new and exciting to me. Just look at them," she said, pointing to the busy employees. "Everyone works together to get it all done. Does it ever stop?"

"For a while, in the late mornings when the casino

crowd settles down," he answered. "And speaking of them, I need to get back there."

"Is that the chef?" she asked, pointing to a large man in a tall, white hat.

"Right, that's Charles. Come on," he said, "I'll introduce you to him."

She took a step back. "Oh! I don't want to bother him."

"You won't. I came in to speak to him, anyway."

He slipped his hand around her waist as he led her through the bustling room to the man. The gesture made her feel safe, but she knew better than to trust her instincts and ignored the ripple that chased through her body.

"Carly, this is Charles, the Devil's Den's famous chef," Dev said when they'd reached the man's side. "Charles, I'd like you to meet Carly. She's a special guest of mine and was quite delighted with her breakfast."

"It was wonderful," Carly said, extending her hand.

"*Bonsoir, mademoiselle*," he answered, taking her hand and brushing his lips across it. "*Je suis heureux de savoir que vous avez apprécié mes créations du matin.*"

She glanced over her shoulder and grinned at Dev before answering Charles. "*Vous êtes très bienvenu, mais c'était mon plaisir.*"

Dev smiled at the two of them. "I had a feeling you two would hit it off, even if I don't understand everything you said."

Carly sneaked a look at Charles before translating. "He said he's glad I liked it, and I said it was my pleasure."

Charles beamed. "She is a delight, Devon," he said

with a heavy accent. "Thank you for bringing her to me." Looking at Carly, he released her hand. "It has been *my* pleasure, but I must get back to my work, *mademoiselle*."

"*Merci*, Charles," she answered.

"If you'll give me a minute, Carly," Dev said, "I'll be right with you."

She understood he had business to tend to, but she itched to know what it might be. Moving back to her corner, she waited until Dev finished and approached her again.

"I'm glad I found you," he said, leading her out of the noisy kitchen and into the hallway. "I wanted to tell you that I'll have a busy night and probably won't see you until dinner tomorrow. Will you be all right?"

Carly felt a stab of regret that she would have to entertain herself while he worked, but she shoved it aside. Dev was a businessman, and she had no right to interfere or expect him to entertain her.

"Yes, I'll be fine."

He nodded. "Order whatever you'd like from room service in the morning. I'll try to stop by later in the afternoon, if I can."

"Don't worry about me," she said, laying her hand on his arm. But she quickly withdrew it when she felt the flush of heat on her face. Touching people she knew was a habit, and she reminded herself that she didn't know him all that well.

"Then I'll see you tomorrow at dinner," he said.

She watched him walk away, feeling a little lost and lonely. It was a pity she enjoyed his company so much. But she had enjoyed James's, too, and look where it had led her. She would be much wiser to err on the side of caution. There was no telling how long she would stay at the Devil's Den, and she suspected that the longer she stayed, the harder it would be to leave.

"Sorry I'm late," Dev said as he stepped inside his suite the next evening. "Did Charles—"

"Isn't it beautiful?"

He was struck speechless. Carly stood next to the small table, which was covered with a lacy white cloth, topped with an arrangement of delicate flowers and flickering candles. Beside the table, a cart was loaded with covered dishes.

He cleared his throat. "Yes," he finally managed to say. "Yes, it is." But he wasn't sure what was more beautiful, the table or the woman standing next to it. Charles was matchmaking. No doubt about it. But Dev didn't need any help. In fact, he needed help getting Carly *out* of his mind. She had haunted his thoughts since he had left her in the hallway outside the hotel kitchen. If he hadn't been so busy with the casino and the details of the sale, he would have checked on her. But as it was, he hadn't had a free moment for almost twenty-four hours.

He tore his gaze away from the scene. He had learned one important thing as they'd shared dinner the night before. Candlelight and Carly Albright were deadly to a man's soul. And his soul was definitely in danger. He hoped a shower would help.

"Charles certainly outdid himself," he said as he went to the bedroom. "If you'll give me a few minutes, I'll get cleaned up and we can have dinner. I won't be long."

He didn't bother to wait for her answer, concentrating instead on the thought of the stinging spray. Too many hours and no sleep had left him feeling like he was walking through a haze. If it wasn't for Carly waiting to share dinner, he would try for a short nap. But it would have had to be short. He still had early rounds to make and the rest of the night ahead.

His reflection, as he looked in the mirror, brought him up short. It was a good thing they would be eating by candlelight. His eye was red and bloodshot from lack of sleep. He needed a shave. He needed a shower.

When he had finished, both had him feeling halfway human again. Checking first to make sure Carly wasn't in the bedroom, he hurried to dress. He was just about to button his shirt when there was a soft knock on the door.

"There's someone here with a message for you," Carly said from the other side.

Rejuvenated by his shower, he had been looking forward to a quiet dinner, in spite of the distraction Carly posed. But business came first. With a sigh, he walked to the bedroom door and opened it.

Carly's gaze went straight to his bare chest and then slid up to meet his. He had to bite the inside of his cheek to keep from grinning. It served her right. He was sure he'd had the same look on his face more than once when looking at her.

Glancing toward the door to the suite, he saw one of his security officers. "I'll only be a minute," he told Carly and began to button his shirt.

Lloyd didn't raise an eyebrow as Dev approached. If nothing else, the Devil's Den employees were well trained. Not that Dev was often seen with a woman, but they knew the meaning of discreet. They had to, working in a casino where some of the wealthiest people in the area were sometimes known to lose their shirts. Both buttoned and unbuttoned.

"Sorry, sir. I should've just called, but Greg thought it best to tell you in person."

"What is it, Lloyd?"

"Mr. Staton has been seen at the Horseshoe."

Dev looked around to make sure Carly wasn't listening and saw that her back was turned as she went through the small refrigerator behind the bar. "Is he still there?" he asked the man.

Lloyd shook his head. "They weren't able to get word to him about your, uh, guest, either. He was only there for a few minutes."

"Any other reports from the other casinos?"

"No, sir."

Dev wasn't sure what to think. Either J.R. was looking for Carly, or he had just arrived in town with no idea that she was in Shreveport. But Dev would've bet the Devil's Den that J.R. saw Carly leave the church with him. What was taking J.R. so long? Was he playing games to keep them off guard?

"Are you staying for dinner?" Carly asked when Dev had closed the door behind the man.

"Of course. Why wouldn't I?"

"You're so busy," she said with a small shrug.

Dev had to swallow around the lump of guilt that suddenly formed in his throat. He had brought her here without giving much thought as to what would happen. That wasn't at all like him. Except for the poker game that had won him the Devil's Den, he didn't do things by chance. He planned and he worked for what he wanted. And he didn't give up. His father was proof of that. If he hadn't been so hell-bent on leaving the ranch and arguing with his dad about it the morning— He shook the memory from his mind. Time enough for that later.

"Not too busy to have dinner with you," he told Carly. He joined her at the table and pulled out her chair. "What did Charles send us?"

"More than both of us can eat, I'm sure," she answered with a laugh. Settling in the chair he held for her, she looked up to smile at him.

There was no way in hell he could keep from reacting to that sweet, sexy smile, so he returned one of his own and quickly turned his attention to the cart of food. But it was hard to concentrate on the dishes that Charles and the kitchen staff had prepared. Carly's sweet smile haunted him.

Without looking at her, he asked, "Where do you want to start?"

"I didn't even peek, so what are the choices?"

Without thinking, he rattled off the long list of appetizers, soups, salads and main dishes, wishing he had just stayed down in the casino instead of subjecting himself to this quiet, intimate dinner. He had been working too hard. Not getting enough sleep. Carly might be easy on the eyes, but she was an innocent, and he had never had a penchant for that kind of woman. In a matter of days, he would tire of her naiveté, and life would be back to normal. He hoped.

Carly made her choices, and he placed them on the

table. "Did you have fun today?" he asked, taking his seat across from her.

"You know, I really did," she said, spreading the snowy linen napkin in her lap. "You really have great people working for you. And they like you."

He looked up to stare at her. "They do?"

"Oh, yes, everyone I met had nice things to say about you."

He didn't doubt that Charles would say nice things. But the rest of the staff? Then again, Shirley had always said the staff was like family. And he had to admit that many of them had taken the place of his own family, even though he had never felt he was all that close to them.

"Who is 'everyone'?" he asked, curious to know whom she had met.

She stopped the fork of salad halfway to her mouth. "Well, let me think." Placing the fork on her plate, she tilted her head to the side. "David was the first I met. He's the waiter who came for our cart last night after you left and took me down to the kitchen."

"Took you?"

Her cheeks flushed a pretty pink. "To be honest, I followed him at first, but I assured him that he wouldn't get in trouble. He won't, right?"

"Right," he answered. David had worked for him since the beginning, hired because he had gotten a young girl pregnant and was ordered by the court to get a job. Dev had never been disappointed in him. "So you met David and Charles. Is that all?"

"Oh, no. There's Janice in housekeeping and Todd in security and—"

"Todd Atkins?"

Her eyes narrowed in thought, but quickly brightened. "Yes. That's his name."

Dev made a mental note to remind Todd and the others in security that they were not to mention J.R. to Carly. Although she was here of her own free will, that free will was limited by not having anywhere else to go. In truth, he was taking advantage of her, hoping J.R. would come to find her. And Dev didn't know how she might react if she knew.

"Everyone said nice things about you," she continued.

"Exactly how many people did you meet on your, uh, adventure?"

"Lots. I can't even remember everyone's name," she said with a grin. "And they were all as nice as could be. Kate even showed me how to make the beds. She does such a good job. I never knew there was a trick to make it go faster. And easier."

Dev could only nod. He imagined there were secrets to doing things better that even he didn't know. But *lots*? She must have spent all day wandering the hotel. Then again, she hadn't had much else to do, so he shouldn't be surprised. If he had more time, he would be happy to keep her company. At that moment she was enjoying the dinner Charles had prepared for them. It seemed that Carly enjoyed just about everything.

"I'm glad you had a good time and made so many friends," he told her honestly.

"I really did. Thank you for letting me."

The idea struck him that if he weren't selling the business, he would hire her. In time, that might be a solution, although he didn't see her as the type to be making beds and emptying trash bins. She was good with people, evidenced by how fast she made friends. And that could be a problem.

But no bigger problem than what faced him as he sat across the table from her. Simply looking at her had him fighting the urge to kiss her again. Doing that was totally out of the question. And damned hard to resist. The sooner J.R. arrived, whether looking for her or not, the sooner Dev would have him apprehended and could then concentrate on other matters. The sale of the business, for one thing. How to help Carly, for another.

Tired from spending another morning of roaming the hotel hallways, Carly opened the door to the suite and walked in. "Oh! You're here."

Dev was hanging up the phone and turned to look at her. "I was just asking around for you."

Taking a seat on the long sofa, she leaned back and closed her eyes. "My feet hurt from walking so much, so I decided to take a break." She turned to look at him behind her. "Will you be here long?"

"For a while." He joined her on the other end of the sofa. "How many more of my employees did you meet this morning?" he asked, with his devastating grin.

"How many do you have?" she countered, returning the grin.

"You know, I'm not sure of the exact number, but enough to keep the place running smoothly." He hesitated. "Most of the time."

"But you have to work so hard and spend time keeping an eye on the casino. Is it worth it?"

"It has been."

She wasn't sure what to make of his answers. She knew so very little about him, except that he had two brothers, and she guessed they might be in Texas, although he had never said. "How long have you owned the Devil's Den?"

"Full of questions today, aren't you?"

"And you're answering my question with a question," she pointed out. "I'm losing ground."

Throwing his head back, he laughed. "And I apologize. It's been mine for three years."

"You bought it three years ago? Was it as busy then as it is now?"

"Not nearly. I was working for a drilling company, and we played a lot of poker to make time go by when we couldn't work. Out in the middle of nowhere, there isn't always a lot to do."

She was amazed that she had him talking, and decided this would be the opportune time to question him more. "Kind of like me here?"

"Maybe not so bad."

"And?"

"And the owner of what was then the Lucky Star happened to walk into the bar where we were playing and joined us. It was a little place, and maybe he thought he'd have some luck."

"But he didn't?"

His smile broadened. "He was the worst poker player I'd ever met. Before we knew it, he was in deep. And I was winning big. When it came down to the last hand, all he had left was this place. I didn't know it at the time, but the Lucky Star was losing money hand over fist."

"You won the Devil's Den in a poker game? So you *are* a gambler, after all." It was news she wasn't happy to hear, but she wasn't surprised, either. Hadn't she suspected it?

"My mom and dad were both big poker players," he said with a shrug. "Especially my mom. She loved it. Taught my older brother and me when we could barely talk. But if you think this place was a great prize, you're wrong. It was next to falling apart when I bought it. It took me most of a year to bring it and its clientele up to par."

She stared at him. "Amazing."

"And before you ask," he went on, "about half the employees I have now came with the deal."

"So you hired more?"

"I had to. Business boomed."

"How is it now?"

"What do *you* think?"

Judging by the crowds in the casino, Carly was pretty certain business was good. And if she judged the owner by what his employees said about him, she would conclude that he was a generous boss. But she had learned that from her own experience.

"It's still booming," she answered. "Probably because you're so generous. I don't know how to thank you for helping me."

He shifted on the sofa. "You don't need to."

"But I don't understand why you did it. Except that you knew James."

"Somebody had to, and it didn't look like you were going to get much help at the church."

"That's it?" she asked, surprised that there wasn't

more. He hadn't known her then, hadn't known that what she had said was true.

"Pretty much."

Knowing firsthand how generous he had been with her, Carly believed there wasn't anything else to the story. He had seen her, lent his assistance, and the rest was pretty much history. But she had one question.

"Why were you there?" she asked. "Why attend the wedding of a man who obviously isn't a good friend?"

Dev shrugged and stretched his arms across the back of the sofa. "Curiosity. I happened to be in Baton Rouge and learned about it."

She gave an absentminded nod, thinking of what might have happened if he hadn't been there. Of where she might be now and if she might have been swayed to return and finish the ceremony.

"What I'm wondering," Dev said, breaking into her thoughts, "is what you planned to do after you left the church."

"Nothing," she said, wincing at the thought of her usual impulsiveness. "I was so worried about what everyone would do, I didn't think any further." She could feel her throat thickening with threatening tears at the memory of that awful moment. "It was clear that James didn't love me as much as I'd thought, but any more than that…" She shook her head, unable to say more.

Dev moved closer and pulled her next to him. "It was pretty bad, huh?"

All she could do was nod. It wasn't like her to get all emotional. She rarely cried. Tears had no purpose in her life. But she was feeling sorry for herself and at loose ends. If only she had an idea of what she should do or where she would go, when it was time to leave Dev's care.

"Would you like me to take you home?" he asked.

She shook her head. "Not yet. I just can't. And I'm sorry to be such a burden to you."

He leaned back and looked at her. "You aren't a burden."

Sighing, she wondered how she had been so fortunate to have him show up at her wedding. But it was time to start making some plans for the future. And there was no time like the present.

"I think I should look for a job," she stated.

"A job?" he asked.

"Yes. As in gainfully employed."

"Why?"

It was her turn to stare at him. "I think a more appropriate question would be, Why not. I have to do something. I can't stay here forever."

"In time, a job would be a good idea. I think I can help you with it," he said, moving away and standing. "You're dealing with a lot of stuff. Why not give yourself a little more time to adjust to what is obviously a new way of life for you? Unless there's a reason you don't want to stay here for a little while longer."

"No, that isn't it," she cried. The more she thought about it, the more she believed he might be right. If she continued to spend time talking with the employees of the Devil's Den, she might learn enough from them to find a job here in Shreveport. Maybe she could eventually become a dealer. She had heard there was good money in that.

"All right," she relented. "I see your point."

"Then it's settled." He took a few steps away and then turned back. "Stop worrying about it, Carly. Everything will work out."

Since she didn't have a basis for an argument, she nodded. Standing, she squared her shoulders. "If it's all right, I think I'll go see what Charles is planning for dinner tonight."

"Good idea," he answered. "Take your time. I think I'll try to catch a short nap."

She crossed the room to the door, not sure if she was happy about the outcome of their little talk, or whether things had changed at all. "I'll see you at dinner then," she said, opening the door. Giving a halfhearted wave, she stepped out into the hallway and closed the door behind her.

By all accounts, Devon Brannigan was a good man. But she had misjudged James. Was she trusting Dev too much, unable to see him clearly because she was too attracted to him? And what would happen if that attraction became more? What if she were to fall in love with him?

Chapter Five

When Carly had gone, Dev stretched out on the sofa, hoping for a short nap. But in spite of having had next to no sleep, he couldn't seem to shut off his mind. He couldn't imagine anyone doing what Carly had done without some kind of plan or even an idea of what to do. Calling off her wedding at the last possible moment *had* been a plan, but even she admitted that it had stopped there. He didn't operate like that. Didn't live his life on the edge. Even when he had won the Lucky Star, he had begun to plan immediately.

For him, everything needed a plan to run smoothly. When it came to Carly, his plan had changed when he'd taken her from the church, but it had meant an adjustment, nothing more. It all came down to his goal of getting back home to the Triple B. But to do that, he had to sell the Devil's Den first. Then he would have to come clean to his brothers about the cause of their father's sudden heart attack sixteen years before. If Chace and Trey turned him away, he would have nowhere to go. Much the same as Carly. At least he had skills. He just didn't want to think about what he would do if his brothers turned him away. For him the future was a huge blank.

Wide awake and feeling guilty about taking advantage of Carly, he decided to do something special for her. She needed something to wear besides his old sweats and the one dress he had picked out for her. A quick call to the kitchen netted him the information he needed. Carly was talking to Charles.

He left immediately and after a short stop at the security office to check on the activities in the casino he found Carly as she was leaving the kitchen. Taking her by the arm, he guided her in the direction of the hotel lobby.

"Where are we going?" she asked, obviously surprised to see him.

"Shopping."

She looked up at him, her eyes narrowed. "For what?"

His gaze traveled from her feet to the top of her head. "Shoes, jeans, shirts, dresses, whatever you need."

"Unmentionables?" she asked, her grin wicked.

"If you need them," he said with a shrug. "If you want them."

She came to a stop in the middle of the lobby. "I can't let you do it, Dev."

Letting go of her arm, he turned to face her. The look on her face nearly brought him to his knees. Even though her mouth was set in a firm, stubborn line, her eyes shimmered with what he suspected were tears. He wasn't sure whether to take a hard stand with her and insist she let him buy her some new clothes or whether he should follow his natural instincts and pull her into his arms to kiss her senseless.

He chose the former.

"If you feel it's necessary to pay me back sometime in the future, I won't stop you," he told her. Taking her arm again, he urged her to follow him. "Until then I would feel better if you had something more to wear than the dress you have on, a swimsuit, and a pair of sweats that make you look like someone washed you and you shrunk."

"Don't forget my wedding gown."

He felt her relax and give in to his argument. Damn good thing she did. It wasn't that kissing her was a bad thing. It was the stopping the kissing that gave him trouble.

At the door to the hotel's exclusive shop, he released her, promising himself he wouldn't let her go overboard—not this time, anyway—and following her inside.

"Hi, Carly," Janet, the shop's manager, called out to her.

Dev should have been surprised that even Janet knew Carly, but he wasn't. Carly had made good use of her free time.

"What can I help you with, Mr. Brannigan?" Janet asked.

"A few things for Carly." He pulled a shirt from a rack and considered it. "She needs a few basic things.

Shirts, pants, a few dresses. Oh, and some shoes," he added, replacing the shirt.

Janet nodded, but before he could say more, his cell phone rang. Pulling it out, he gave them both an apologetic smile and turned to walk to a corner of the shop. "Brannigan," he answered.

"I'm sorry to bother you, Mr. Brannigan," Shirley said, "but you said to call you immediately if another bid came in."

"I'll be right there." Stuffing the phone back into its holder, he turned to the two women. "I hope you can do without me for a while. Get whatever you need Carly. Janet will take care of the tab for me."

"But—" Carly began.

"I won't be long, and I'll check to see if you're still here when I'm done. If not, I'll see you back in the suite." He didn't wait to hear her reply. She was in good hands with Janet, and he was eager to see this latest bid.

In his office Shirley handed him an envelope. "I hope it's a good one," she said, settling back at her desk.

"There's still the one that came the other day," he answered, tearing it open and pulling out the paper. With only two days left until the bidding closed, he was looking forward to being done with this part of the sale.

His eyes widened as he read the figure in the letter. It was definitely over the top. Someone was willing to spend a small fortune to own the Devil's Den. He couldn't blame the person. The place was worth a small fortune.

Taking a key ring from his pocket, he smiled. Of the

several bids he had received, the last two were the most generous. He unlocked his desk drawer and slipped the envelope into the folder with the others. It wouldn't be long before the Devil's Den belonged to someone else.

"Thanks, Shirley." He stood and walked around his desk, heading for the door. "There may be a few more yet, before the deadline."

"It was good?" she asked.

"Very good." Offering her a smile, he left the office, feeling more than pleased. J.R. had been in the area, which meant that soon he would have J.R. dealt with, as well as the sale. Then he would return to the ranch. Once he talked to his brothers, he could focus his attention on his future, whatever it might be. And Carly.

"What do you think?" Carly held her breath as she made a slow circle to show Dev another of the items she had found in the hotel shop. This one, a gaily flowered creation that swirled around her legs, was her favorite of the lot.

"I think you have great taste," he said, meeting her gaze with his own. An appreciative gleam sparkled in his eyes. "And it's obvious that you didn't need me to help at all."

By the look he was giving her, she wondered if maybe she hadn't gone a bit overboard. The scoop neck of the dress was much lower than what she would normally choose. But the dress was a dreamy concoction of sheer, spring-flowered fabric over a peach shade that did great things for her auburn hair.

"You're sure it isn't a little…" she asked, looking down at the neckline.

"Not a bit." He closed the distance between them, stopping a mere foot from where she stood. "And it looks much better on you than it did on the hanger in the shop. Much."

Carly felt her cheeks heat with a blush as she lifted her gaze to his. "It's a bit dressy, but I couldn't resist." Reaching out, she touched his arm. "I can't thank you enough. Everything is wonderful. I mean, I didn't buy a lot, but what I did should go a long way. Janet was good enough to steer me to the discount rack."

"She didn't need to do that," he said, reaching up to tuck a wayward strand of hair from her face.

Her heartbeat quickened at his touch, and she absent-mindedly tucked the lock securely behind her ear. "I…I sort of explained to her that we were old friends and you were helping me out of a jam until I could get on my feet again. Which I hope will be soon," she added quickly.

"Then you were honest about it."

"Well, except for the old friends part," she admitted.

"Almost honest, then."

The way he was looking at her stopped her breath. His blue eyes had darkened to navy, but he hadn't moved an inch. Still, somehow he felt closer with every breath she managed to drag in.

"H—have you had any sleep?" she was able to ask. Her voice sounded low and lazy.

"Not much," he said with a slight shrug, but his gaze never left hers. "How about you? How are you sleeping?"

She could barely move, but managed a small nod. "Fine. The suite is very quiet. I forget this is a busy hotel with a casino. But I guess you know that."

"The...bed...is comfortable?"

The way he said it sent a warmth of pleasure through her. His voice was deep. Seductive. And she couldn't stop hoping that he would kiss her again. "Very," she answered, her own voice a whisper.

He raised his hand to brush his knuckles along her cheek. "Good. Some people might feel it was too..."

"Hard?" She immediately wished she hadn't provided the word. "N-no, not at all. It's firm, yet..." She was getting in deeper with every word she spoke. It was time to be quiet. Maybe then he would put her out of her misery and kiss her.

For an endless eternity she waited. But instead of the kiss she was hoping for, he dropped his hand and turned to walk to the sofa, where he sat, leaning back with his arms stretched along the back.

From her vantage point, all she could see was the back of his head, with no way to guess at what he might be thinking or feeling. She was thoroughly disappointed in herself. Was she so unattractive that he couldn't manage a repeat of their earlier kiss? Or was it that he just didn't like her? Kissing him would be wrong, she knew, considering her poor judgment, but she didn't care. She kept hoping. Her Southern upbringing had taught her that she couldn't come right out and ask him to take her in his arms. Flirt, yes. Brazenly request, heavens no!

With a heavy sigh, she turned for the bedroom. "I guess I'll go change," she called to him. He raised his hand in answer but didn't say anything. Discouraged, and torn between being good and enjoying what most young women her age found natural, she entered the bedroom. She put away her new clothes and changed into a pretty pink top that barely skimmed the waistband of her new jeans.

Checking her hair in the bathroom mirror, she had a thought. Maybe he needed some encouragement. Maybe just standing there, looking at him and hoping, wasn't enough. Maybe he didn't know she wanted him to kiss her again.

Determined to find a way—any way without actually coming on to him—to let him know she wasn't averse to the idea of kissing him again, Carly returned to the living room where she found Dev rummaging through the small refrigerator behind the bar.

"Looking for something special?" she asked as she walked to stand beside him. Wincing when his head hit the edge of the bar, she lost her nerve. This wasn't the time for kisses. "Sorry. I didn't mean to surprise you."

He rubbed the top of his head as he straightened and faced her. "My fault. I was lost in thought."

Carly hoped he had been thinking about her, but she doubted it. He was a busy businessman, with much more to think about than a runaway bride who would probably cost him a small fortune before she was able to make it on her own and pay him back.

Without thinking, she stood on tiptoe. "Thank you again, Dev," she said as she stretched to kiss him on his cheek.

"Carly…"

Her name was more a sigh than a word on his lips

as he grasped her waist, his fingers burning the skin
bared by her short top. She closed her eyes and held
back the gasp that his touch caused.

Slowly he pulled her closer. "You're playing with
fire," he said, his breath whispering across her cheek.

"Probably," she managed to say. Placing her hands on
his shoulders, she opened her eyes and looked into his
and waited. Again. Only this time she wasn't disappointed.

When his lips touched hers, she was afraid she would
faint at the tenderness she felt. Unlike the first kiss they
had shared, he gently brushed his mouth on hers in a
tentative teasing. She didn't pull away. Instead she
slipped her hands around his neck and leaned into him.
Hussy, she could hear *Mamère* saying. But Carly knew
that wasn't true. There was nothing wrong with a
woman enjoying a man's kiss. And she intended to
enjoy this one.

Ripples of pleasure flowed through her when he slid
his hands around her, holding her closer as his tongue
teased at her lips. With a soft sigh, she opened, giving
him entry and matching his movements with her own.

She heard his deep moan and thrilled at it. Barely
able to think clearly, her only thought was that she
wasn't so unattractive to him after all. After that, all
thought was gone, as she let herself be swept away by
the sensations he aroused in her.

Just as she was thinking the kiss might never end—
and hoping it wouldn't—he pulled away, leaving her
bereft of the warmth of him and the heat of his kiss.

"I…I need to take care of something," he said,
turning away and striding to the door.

"Dev, I'm—"

"It can't wait." Without another word, he was gone, pulling the door closed behind him.

Carly stared after him. What had she done? Had she said something? No, she hadn't said anything. She knew that. It was what she had done.

Stunned, she made her way slowly to the sofa on legs that would barely hold her and sank onto it. *Mamère* was right. She had acted in an unladylike manner. Maybe not exactly a hussy, because she wasn't and couldn't be, not even for a moment. And, in truth she hadn't even thought, when she had thanked him with her chaste kiss on the cheek, that what had happened would happen, but… But he had stopped, and he had walked away. Again.

Maybe the question she needed to ask herself was why she wanted it so badly. Part of the answer to that was easy. His kisses made her forget her problems. But kissing him—even wanting to kiss him—only made the problems worse. She knew her judgment was severely flawed. Almost marrying James was proof enough of that. Fleeing her wedding with no plan for her future proved how impulsive she was. Falling for Dev—

No. She hadn't fallen for him. Not yet.

Or had she?

That was something she didn't want to think about. She wasn't ready to face the truth. Which was bad. Not facing the truth, when doubt had begun to rear its ugly head, was what had led her to continue with her wedding plans. She had avoided the issue of James's strange behavior weeks before the wedding by convincing herself that it was her own prewedding jitters, when in fact the truth had been there for her to see and admit.

When she had learned what had happened between Prissy and James, she knew she couldn't go through with the wedding. Not only had James betrayed her, but Prissy, who was supposed to be her best friend, had committed an even bigger betrayal. Fear of what would happen if she called off the wedding the day before it was to take place had led her to do what she had done. But her impulsive nature had kept her from planning any more than that. If it hadn't been for Dev being at the wedding and lending his help—

She brought herself up short. Thinking about things was becoming an obsession. Left alone in Dev's suite and the hotel gave her too much time to think. It was like going in circles. She needed to get out, away from the man who was constantly in her thoughts.

And that's exactly what she would do.

"She did what?" Dev shouted at his head of Security.

Greg didn't flinch. "She left a couple of hours ago."

Dev stared at the wall of monitors in the Security Office, afraid to guess where Carly might have gone. He was pretty sure he knew *why*.

"And where were you when this happened?" he asked, trying his best to control his temper. But whether he was angry at Greg, Carly or himself, he didn't know.

"I was at lunch. Corey was monitoring. He didn't know to alert you immediately. That's my fault. But he did tell me when I came in."

Dev looked at his watch. "She's been gone, what? An hour?"

"Maybe more," Greg admitted. "I had a short meeting with some of the staff after lunch. It's probably been closer to two hours."

Dev wasn't sure what to do. Should he go up to the suite and wait in case she returned? He wasn't completely sure she *would* return. For all he knew, ending their kiss so abruptly had been a sign to Carly that he didn't want her. That he wasn't enjoying the kiss. And that was about as far from the truth as possible. He had been enjoying it too much. Way too much. Just the thought of it turned his blood to fire.

No, he couldn't sit in the suite and wait for her. He would go crazy. And he couldn't go out hunting for her. Where would he look? As far as he knew, she had no money. She couldn't take a bus, a train or even a taxi. She had become a prisoner, not only of the hotel, but of the entire city of Shreveport. And he had done it.

"I'll be on the floor," he told Greg. "Call me if— *when* she returns."

"I'm sorry about this," Greg said as Dev reached the door. "I should've made everyone aware of the situation."

"You did what I told you to do," Dev admitted. "This is my fault, not yours."

Shirley smiled at him as he walked through the outer office, but Dev couldn't offer a smile in return. In the hallway the urge to punch something consumed him immediately, but he managed to fight it off. Hurting his hand and damaging the wall wouldn't bring Carly back. All he could do was hope that she was out for a

breath of fresh air and nothing more. Even with her
having the run of the hotel, he knew she was champing
at the bit for more freedom. She wanted to be self-
sufficient, wanted a job so she could take care of
herself, instead of depending on him. He couldn't
blame her for that. Any more than he could blame her
for thinking he hadn't wanted to kiss her. He had
managed to handle everything very badly. This was his
payback. Worrying about Carly wouldn't bring her
back any sooner. If at all.

Determined to concentrate on business as much as
possible, he spent the next two hours in the casino. He
hadn't slept more than fifteen minutes in the past forty-
eight hours, but until he knew Carly was safe, sleep
was beyond him.

"How's it going?" he asked Greg, when he had
returned to the security room.

"It's quiet."

Dev took the chair next to him and surveyed the
screens in front of him. "No sign of Staton yet? Any
word?"

"Gordon over at the Isle of Capri thought he saw
him earlier today, but then decided it was someone
else."

"He has to be somewhere," Dev muttered. "Did we
find out if he was staying at…" He stared at the
monitor in front of him that covered the front entrance
of the hotel, and relief flooded through him.

"She's back?" Greg asked.

Dev jumped to his feet, almost knocking the chair
over in the process. "She's back."

He hurried out of the offices and was lucky enough

to get an elevator that wasn't in use. At his suite, he was pleased to discover that he had made it there before Carly. It gave him the chance to calm down, before confronting her about scaring him to death.

Taking a seat on the sofa, he breathed in, letting it out in a long whoosh, seconds before the door to the suite opened.

Carly walked in, not noticing him at first. When she did, she stopped, her mouth open and her eyes widened in surprise. "Oh! Hi, Dev," she said, moving quickly in the direction of the bedroom.

Dev had to bite his cheek to keep from laughing. Over the jeans she had purchased earlier that day, she wore a long black shirt that was several sizes too large. Her hair was tucked under a floppy-brimmed straw hat. He was sure she was hoping to avoid him, but he wasn't going to give her that advantage. As calmly as possible, he asked, "Going somewhere?"

She stopped halfway through the sitting room, but didn't turn to look at him. "I…I thought I'd change."

He got to his feet and walked toward her before she could escape. Taking her gently by the arm, he turned her around to face him, careful not to get hit by the brim of her hat. "Where have you been, Carly?"

Her chin went up as she met his gaze. "Out."

"In this outfit?" he asked.

She looked down at her clothes. "I didn't want to be noticed," she admitted, with a trace of reluctance in her voice.

"This is my shirt," he said, touching the collar near her chin, "but where did you get the hat?"

"The shop in the lobby."

"I must have missed seeing it. Why don't we sit down and you can tell me about your adventure."

When they were comfortable on the sofa, she pulled off her hat, and her copper-colored hair tumbled around her shoulders. Dev's breath caught in his chest, but he managed to keep his hands to himself, in spite of wanting to run them through her locks.

He took a deep breath and cleared his throat before speaking. "You know, going out in a strange city by yourself isn't a wise thing to do."

Her head was lowered, concealing her face, but she peeked up from beneath her lashes. "If I had told you I was going, you wouldn't have let me."

"You're right."

"And if I hadn't gone, I wouldn't have had such a wonderful time."

Guilt crept over Dev. He wasn't trying to hold her hostage, though it seemed that way, even to him. "I'm glad you had a good time. But I was worried about you. Shreveport is fairly safe, but you're a stranger and don't know your way around. You don't know the areas to stay away from, where you could find yourself in trouble," he explained.

"I stopped at the concierge desk and asked the best places to see. That were free, of course," she added in a rush. "There were so many places, I didn't visit half of them. I truly didn't mean to worry you. I just needed…to get away."

Dev understood, but he was still concerned. He didn't have the right to keep her from leaving, whether she left for an hour or permanently. On the other hand, he wanted to keep her safe. He wasn't worried about

J.R. hurting her physically. That wasn't J.R.'s style. But she had been hurt emotionally, and he would never forgive himself if he let it happen again. At least while she was in his protection, however long that might be.

"Let me know before you set out on another adventure, okay?" he said as he got to his feet.

"Is it okay if I go down to talk to Charles?"

"Of course. But you might want to wear something besides my shirt," he answered with a smile.

"Good idea," she said with a grin.

When she had gone into the bedroom to change, he stretched out on the sofa. He couldn't deny that he was more than attracted to Carly. But there was nothing he could do about it. With his future still uncertain, a woman was a luxury he couldn't afford. He couldn't commit to a short-term relationship with her, much less anything long-term, and he suddenly wished things could be different.

Chapter Six

"Is everything all right, Mama?"

"Oh, honey, everything is just perfect."

Carly didn't miss the note of excitement in her mother's voice on the phone. The news could be good. Then again, knowing her mother, it could mean anything. "Why?" Carly asked. "Has something happened? Have you found an apartment you like?"

"So many questions, Carly! You'll never believe what's happened. I'm not going to have to move."

A wave of dread swept through Carly. Knowing her mother's current financial state, especially after the money spent on a wedding that didn't happen, she couldn't think of any way her mother would be able to keep Oak Hill. "Mama, I don't know who you've been talking to, but—"

"Now, Carly, you probably don't remember him.

Why, I don't remember that I ever mentioned his name…"

"*His* name?" The dread became a chill that threatened to invade her bones.

"Did I ever tell you about Dodo?" her mother rushed on. "Of course, that isn't really his name. It's Julian Thibodaux, you see. He was one of my beaux so long ago. But he's come back, and he's going to help me keep Oak Hill."

Carly couldn't shake the chill. And she suddenly realized that she had inherited her trusting nature from her mother. It was no wonder *Mamère* had constantly reminded her not to be so impetuous and impulsive. From the sound of it, Lily Mae was falling for a crooked scheme, just as Carly had with James.

"You have to be careful, Mama," she said as kindly as possible. The last thing she wanted to do was frighten her mother. But on the other hand, she didn't want her to be taken in by a fraud, either. "There are men out there who prey on women like us. Look at James. We thought he was a gentleman. He's bad, Mama. Very bad." It hurt to say it, but Carly felt better for it.

On the other end of the line, Lily Mae let out a long sigh. "Yes, we were very wrong about James. But Dodo isn't like that. I've known him forever. And if he hadn't gone away and joined the Coast Guard, I might have married him, instead of your father. He's only been waiting for the right time to step in and help."

Carly sighed. Would she have to leave the Devil's Den to go home to make sure her mother wasn't being hoodwinked? And if she did leave, would she ever see Dev again? "I'm sure he's very nice, but—"

"He's a friend of Cousin Edward. They've been in touch with each other all these years."

"Cousin Edward?" Carly trusted her mother's cousin. He had known for some time about the strain on the finances and had helped her keep things going for longer than she could have done on her own. "Did Cousin Edward tell this man about…"

"About having no money?" her mother finished. "No, he didn't. Cousin Edward has been more than discreet, so don't you worry about that. I told Dodo myself, and he understood. He has his own money, so it doesn't bother him in the least. He plans to take care of everything and doesn't even want his name on the property. He has his own properties. So, Carly, honey, you see? He isn't anything at all like James."

Relief slowly crept over Carly. If this man from her mother's past was indeed the gentleman her mother said he was, Carly was free from worry. For the first time since her father's death, the responsibility of her mother and the finances would be gone. She was free.

"I must tell you that James was here again," her mother went on. "I didn't tell him about our financial situation. He doesn't need to know that."

"No, Mama, he doesn't," Carly agreed, knowing her mother would never reveal the truth to someone she didn't trust. And now that she had seen what kind of man James was—

"I nearly forgot that he asked me to give you a message."

Carly focused on what her mother was saying. "A message?"

"Yes. He said to be very careful of some man that

you know and not to trust him. Who would that be, Carolyn? And where are you? Fanny Gaspard said you left the church with a man."

"I'm fine, Mama," Carly said, before her mother could ask anything more. She wasn't ready to explain about Dev. "I'm safe. The man who helped me at the church found me a place to stay."

"But where *are* you?"

Asked directly, Carly couldn't lie. "I'm in Shreveport," she answered, but she couldn't say more. She didn't want her mother or Cousin Edward coming to look for her, and she certainly didn't want to see James. "I really need to say goodbye, for now. I'll call you again. Soon."

Before her mother could say another word, Carly ended the conversation. Leaning back against the bed pillow, she closed her eyes, hoping to sort things out. She didn't like that James had been to see her mother a second time and he obviously knew where she was. If Dev was telling the truth about him—and she was convinced he was—James's warning was practically a threat. He might foolishly think she would run away from Dev and right into his arms, but that wouldn't happen, no matter what she did or where she went. It was no wonder Dev was being so protective. She had proven that she did things without thinking them through. If she hadn't met him, there was no telling what might have happened to her.

Not wanting to dwell on something that made her sad, she decided she needed a diversion. She hadn't seen the entire hotel yet, and there was no time like the present to continue her wandering.

Noticing Dev was gone from the sitting room, she quickly scribbled a note so he wouldn't be worried that she had left the hotel again. In the elevator she pressed the second-floor button. She had been so busy meeting the employees on the main floor that she had never checked out what might be on that floor.

When she came to a door marked with Dev's name, she turned the handle, expecting to find a large, plush office, in keeping with the style of his suite. She wasn't disappointed when she stepped inside, where a slightly graying woman sat at a large desk, surrounded by comfy-looking club chairs.

"Can I help you, miss?" the woman asked, her smile infectious.

Carly returned the smile. "I'm Carly Albright," she said, hoping Dev had mentioned her name.

The woman stood and leaned over the desk to offer her hand. "Miss Albright, it's good to meet you. I'm Shirley, Mr. Brannigan's secretary." She motioned to a chair near the desk. "Have a seat, won't you? Tell me what you think of the Devil's Den."

"Please, call me Carly." Liking Shirley immediately, she settled on the chair. "I haven't been in the casino much. Dev—I mean Mr. Brannigan—doesn't want me in the there, but I've probably seen just about everything else. It's so busy here, but it runs so smoothly, I'm amazed."

Shirley nodded. "Mr. Brannigan is a genius."

"Everyone seems to like him, too."

"I can't think of a single employee who doesn't," Shirley answered with a gleam of pride in her blue eyes. "Oh, sure, some would like better wages or more days off, or something else, but all in all, they're happy. It would be hard not to be, with a boss who's fair and listens to each of them. If only—" She shook her head.

"If only what?" Carly asked, her curiosity aroused by the worried frown on the woman's face.

"Nothing," Shirley said with a little laugh. "Isn't there always something else we all want?"

Never having worked at a job, Carly couldn't imagine, but when it came to life, she had to agree. She knew that in the not too distant future, she would have to leave Dev and the Devil's Den. She couldn't stay with him permanently, especially when she wasn't sure she could convince him to hire her. He was generous and caring, but as yet he wasn't willing to talk to her about the possibility of employment at the Devil's Den.

And maybe it was for the best. Leaving his protection was inevitable, and although it wouldn't be easy, she needed to deal with the possibility. She would miss him terribly. She was becoming too attached to him. In fact, she was afraid she was falling in love with him.

"Thanks, Steve," Dev told one of his security men in one of the back hallways of the hotel. "I'll have Greg check on it."

"Wait a sec, Dev," Steve said as he grabbed the ringing cell phone strapped to his waist. "What is it?" he asked the caller.

Dev waited to make certain the call wasn't something he needed to attend to. He expected J.R. to appear at any time. Word had it that he was in Shreveport. Whether that was a "still" in town or an "in town again," Dev wasn't sure. What he was sure of was that J.R. would eventually come looking for Carly at the Devil's Den.

"Lloyd just spotted Staton coming in the door," Steve said, slipping his phone back in the holder.

Surprised, even though he had just been wondering when J.R. would arrive, Dev realized that Carly could be anywhere. "Get down there," he ordered. If his men could keep J.R. contained, he could find Carly to make sure she wouldn't be involved, and then he would call the authorities. "I have to take care of something first, but I'll meet you down there."

Without waiting for an answer, Dev hurried along the hallway. There was no telling where Carly might be. When he had left the suite, she was still in the bedroom. He quickly dialed the number for his suite, but after several rings he gave up. He would try the office first. The security cameras might catch her if she was anywhere in the building. And he hoped to hell she was, as long as she wasn't anywhere near the casino.

He was halfway inside the office to check the monitors when he saw her sitting by Shirley's desk. "Carly," he said, relief filling him. "You're here."

She was looking at him, and her eyes widened. "Yes. It's all right, isn't it?"

"Sure, sure," he said, starting for the door where he had come in. Now that he knew Carly was safe, he was needed in the casino. "I'll catch up with you later. There's something I need to take care of."

"Oh, okay, I'll…"

He stepped out into the hall and closed the door behind him, missing the rest of what she was saying.

His mind was on confronting J.R. and putting him where he belonged. But the moment he stepped out of the elevator on the ground floor, he knew something was wrong.

"He slipped out," Lloyd said when Dev reached the three men standing in the lobby.

"Damn." Dev knew J.R. was slippery, but he had counted on catching him this time. "We're going to have to do something about this," he muttered, more to himself than the others.

"We had him," Steve said, looking worried and angry at the same time. "At least we thought we did."

"Someone hit a jackpot," Lloyd explained, "and in that split second that our attention was diverted, he was out the door and gone."

For Dev it was a huge disappointment. He had been waiting for months to catch J.R., but it obviously wasn't time yet. "We'll get him next time," he told the men. "I should've come straight down here, instead of— We'll get him next time."

On his way back to the suite, he mentally kicked himself for checking on Carly before taking care of grabbing J.R. But he knew he hadn't had a choice. He would eventually catch the weasel, but making sure Carly was safely out of what could have been a messy situation had to be his first priority. Was he right in not telling her everything? Or was he more like J.R. than he had thought by using her as a lure?

Except for her brief sightseeing outing, she had been cooped up in the hotel for days. She had become such a part of the place that no one questioned who she was or why she was there. And he had been so intent on getting the sale of the hotel underway that he hadn't stopped to spend much time with her. The sale was important, and the first step to being able to go back to the ranch. Once that was taken care of and J.R. dealt with, he could face what he had avoided for sixteen years. And Carly was stuck in the middle.

He opened the door to the suite and walked in to find Carly standing at the window, her back to him. She looked so vulnerable, he felt guilty for not being a better host. A host who was, in a sense, holding her as hostage, even though being there wasn't against her will.

"Put that new dress on," he told her.

She spun around, facing him. "What? Why?"

"We're going out to see the sights and have a nice dinner somewhere besides here in the room."

Her face lit up like sunshine. "Really?"

"Really. How soon can you be ready?"

Dev watched Carly pick at her meal and wondered what was bothering her. They'd had a pleasant evening, and even if J.R. had seen them and followed them, he knew the scoundrel wouldn't have the nerve to approach them.

"So you met Shirley," he said, hoping some conversation about his secretary would bring her out of whatever funk she was in.

Looking up, she smiled. "She's very nice. And she thinks a lot of you, by the way."

"She's one nice lady," he replied, refilling her wineglass. "She's really the one who keeps everything running smoothly. The Devil's Den would be in trouble if Shirley ever left."

"Even though I didn't spend that much time talking to her today, I couldn't imagine her doing that."

Neither could Dev. With the change in ownership so near, he hoped she wouldn't. He had two excellent bids and sincerely hoped the one he chose would be the best for his employees. If things were different, he wouldn't be selling the property. He hadn't been crazy about becoming the owner, but over the three years the Den had been his, he had grown to care about the place and the people there. But his responsibility was to his family. To tell them the truth.

"Did you meet anyone else today?" he asked, hoping to forget about the uncertainty of the future for the time being.

She shook her head and leaned back in her chair, her gaze lowered as she placed her hands in her lap. Dev knew the look well. "You aren't still thinking that I'm upset about your little adventure today, are you?"

Her only reply was a shake of her head.

Placing his fork on his plate and his linen napkin beside it, Dev leaned forward. In the lowered lights of the restaurant, she looked more vulnerable than usual. He had brought her out to ease his guilt, and here she was, making him feel even guiltier.

"What's wrong?" he asked, reaching across the table to tip her chin up with his finger.

She finally raised her gaze to his, but it was accompanied by a sigh. "I talked to my mama today."

Dev slid his hand up to cup her cheek in his palm, but he quickly pulled away, fighting the urges that were trying to rule him. "Bad news?" he asked, leaning back in his chair to gain restraint of his reactions to her.

"Is she having problems selling the house or finding an apartment?"

"She's not selling."

In the flicker of the candlelight between them, he could see the confusion and concern in her eyes. "Why not?"

She shrugged, as if nothing was bothering her. "Apparently someone from her past has come to help."

"And that worries you?"

"At first it did." She picked a slender breadstick from the basket on the table and twirled it in her fingers. "My first thought was that she was being taken in by someone like…" She looked up, and the breadstick stilled as their gazes caught and held. "She heard from him again."

"James."

Nodding, she began twirling again, intently watching the breadstick move between her fingers. "He had a message for me. He said to be careful and not to trust you."

Except for the first few moments in his Jeep after he had helped her from the church, he had never seen her this withdrawn. J.R. had done what he had intended to do with his message. He had put doubt in Carly's mind. And Dev wasn't sure how to handle that.

"Can we leave now?" she asked, dropping the breadstick to her plate.

Having finished his own meal, Dev nodded and motioned for the waiter. There would be a horse-drawn carriage waiting outside to take them to see the sights of the city at night. But with Carly having withdrawn into herself, he wasn't sure she would even notice, much less enjoy it.

Standing, he stepped around the table and helped her with her chair. *Damn J.R.!* He missed Carly's bubbly love for life. No matter what it took, he would never let J.R. have the chance to con her or anyone else again.

Carly sank beneath the surface of the pool, enjoying the soothing feel of the water on her skin. If only it could wash away her feelings for Dev.

The night before, he had taken her on a tour of the city in a carriage. But she had been so lost in her thoughts, she had barely noticed anything, even the beautiful, high-stepping Percheron pulling it. She hadn't intended for James's message to bother her. She knew Dev, knew he was a kind and generous man. But the message, coupled with knowing her judgment was flawed, had begun to chip away at her confidence in Dev on their way to the restaurant. She had let it ruin their evening. For that she was sorry.

Pushing against the water with her arms, she reached the surface and gasped for air. She wiped the streaming chlorinated water from her eyes and discovered Dev standing at the edge of the pool, watching her. Her heart gave the lurch she had come to expect whenever she was in his company.

"Drowning your sorrows?" he asked.

She smiled, wishing it was that easy. A few strokes took her to the edge, where she looked up at him towering over her in his usual well-tailored black suit. Even with the sun streaming into the room, making it difficult to see clearly, she was well aware of the way he was looking at her. The patch over his eye still reminded her of the devil, but she knew from experience that, when it came to taking care of her, he was an angel.

In a fluid, graceful movement, he knelt and leaned closer.

"You'll get wet," she pointed out.

"I'm okay, as long as you don't decide to share that water with me."

Cupping her hand, she scooped it full of water.

He reached out and grasped her wrist. "I wouldn't," he warned with a wicked grin.

Something like a lightning bolt streaked up her arm and competed with the butterflies doing somersaults in her stomach.

"You still worried about your mother?"

She shook her head, struggling to gain control and find her voice. "Cousin Edward will make sure nothing happens that shouldn't."

For a moment he said nothing. Their gazes locked in a silent conversation she couldn't interpret, until he finally broke it. He released her and stood, giving her the opportunity to take a deep, full breath.

"It promises to be a busy evening," he said, "so maybe we should have dinner early."

"Have you had any sleep?"

"Enough," he answered.

"I doubt it." She knew he kept strange hours, but she also understood that his business dictated it. He might give his secretary credit for everything running smoothly, but Carly knew better. Dev was the real force behind the Devil's Den.

His attention was caught by something outside

the pool area. "I'll see you at dinner," he said, and hurried away.

Carly was relieved to see him go. As much as she enjoyed his company, now wasn't the time. Her heart still pounded from his touch, keeping her from thinking clearly. And she needed to finish sorting through everything that was happening. She just didn't want to.

Turning, she pushed away from the side of the pool and dragged her arms through the water. A few laps and she would feel better, more able to face what she knew she must. She wasn't much of a swimmer. She preferred riding, if given a choice between the two, but any kind of physical exercise would eventually calm her and clear her mind.

After swimming several lengths of the pool, she grew tired and reached for the side, climbing out. She quickly grabbed the towel she'd left on one of the chairs and dried off. Her arms ached from the exercise, but her mind was clear, and she thought about the message her mama had given her from James. She was sure he expected that she would believe him.

Fully aware of how vulnerable she was and on the rebound from a bad situation caused by bad choices, she knew she shouldn't make what she might learn later was an even worse choice. She hoped not. She knew what was in her heart, and it was time to admit that, in spite of her resolve to be cautious where Dev was concerned, she was falling in love with him. Her feelings for him were nothing like she had had for James. The two men were completely different, as were her feelings. But with Dev there was nothing she could do about them.

Feeling better for having admitted the truth, if only to herself, she left the pool area. She held to her bargain and skirted around the casino proper, but her attention was drawn by the noise of the gambling. Glancing to her right, where a long row of slot machines stood, she caught sight of a familiar figure near the blackjack tables.

James.

She quickly hid behind one of the tall, Georgian pillars, while her heart pounded. How ironic that she had just realized and admitted her feelings for Dev at the same time James appeared.

Pressing herself against the cool base of the column, she judged the distance to the bank of elevators. Maybe James would be so intent on the card play that he wouldn't notice her. She prayed she was right. She didn't want to face him. He might be able to convince her, if only for a moment, that she should leave. Even worse, if confronted by him, she might tell him exactly what she thought of him, which would gain her nothing and might possibly anger him.

Determined that James wouldn't see her, she tightened the knot on the towel at her waist, inhaled deeply and watched the bank of elevators for her best chance. The doors on one slid open, depositing several hotel guests, and she made a mad dash for it, just as the doors began to close. She punched the number for the office floor and leaned back against the smooth, polished wood railing as the elevator shot upward.

She would go to the office first. Shirley might know where to find Dev. He knew the circumstances behind her escape from her wedding and also knew that she didn't want to face her once-intended. More now than ever before.

Chapter Seven

"I need to make a decision as soon as possible," Dev told the others at the conference table. "What do we have on this newest bid?"

Sitting at the far end, Lloyd sorted through a folder. "I should have a full dossier on the company before the end of the day."

"Good," Dev answered. Although he would have been happier if he had the information in front of him, he could wait a little longer. He wasn't selling the Devil's Den only for the money, although he hoped to get a lot more than he had put into the place. He wouldn't be a successful businessman if he didn't. But he had promised his employees that the new owner would treat them as they were accustomed to being treated and had added a stipulation to the bidding that would ensure it. The only way to be certain was to check into the bidders, whether they were individuals or corporations.

"Let me know immediately when you have it," Dev told him.

"I'll call—"

"Mr. Brannigan?" Shirley said, opening the door and stepping in from the outer office.

Before Dev had a chance to answer, Carly brushed past her and into the room. "Dev!" she cried, obviously out of breath.

Dev jumped out of his seat and rushed to her side. "What is it, Carly?"

Her gaze darted around the room, taking in the others at the table. "I…I've been looking for you," she said, focusing on him. "It's James."

"He's here?" Dev asked.

Carly nodded, her eyes wide.

Lloyd was on his feet. "I'll get down there," he said as he hurried out of the room. The others followed him.

Guiding Carly to a chair, Dev sat next to her. "You okay?"

She nodded again and took a deep breath, her smile wavering when she answered. "I'm fine. But I thought you'd want to know."

"I do." He didn't want to frighten her. As it was, he wasn't sure if seeing J.R. was the reason for her wide-eyed appearance when she burst into the room or if she had panicked because she hadn't been able to find him. He needed to get down to the casino, but he needed to ask one question more. "Did he see you?"

"I don't think so," she said, shaking her head. "I

was coming from the pool, and I saw him near the blackjack table."

There was no question in Dev's mind that it had been J.R. The man was addicted to blackjack. Hell, he was addicted to any type of gambling. And Carly wouldn't have mistaken someone else for him.

"I ducked behind a column as soon as I noticed him," Carly continued. "Unless he saw me when I made a dash for the elevator."

When she shivered, Dev put his arm around her. A dangerous move, he knew, but he was concerned. "There's no reason to be frightened of him."

"No. He wouldn't hurt me. I know that. But…" She shook her head.

He tipped her chin up with his fingers so he could see her eyes. "But what, sugar?"

"I don't want to talk to him. I don't know what I'd do or what I'd say. I can't deal with him right now."

Fighting the urge to kiss her, Dev removed his arm and stood. "That's understandable."

She looked up at him, her eyes questioning. "Why was Security looking for him?"

He knew this was his chance to tell her the truth, but he couldn't. From her point of view, she would think he had brought her here to lure J.R. to the casino—exactly what he had done. In truth, he hadn't kept her against her will, but he hadn't exactly pushed her out the door, either.

"You looked frightened when you came in," was all he could say. "Lloyd may have thought you felt you were in some kind of danger."

"Oh." She shivered again and rubbed her bare arms. "I guess I should get changed."

Until then he hadn't noticed that she was still in her damp swimsuit and towel. "Might be a good idea," he said, tugging at an equally damp lock of hair. "And I should let you know that I may have to cancel dinner tonight. I've had some unexpected work crop up, and I'll need to get right to it."

Carly pushed away from the table and stood. "Then I probably won't see you until tomorrow. Maybe at breakfast? I think I'll go to bed early tonight."

"You can count on breakfast." He walked with her to the door and out into the reception area. By morning he hoped to have made his decision on the buyer. Deadline for the bidding was midnight, and he didn't want to waste time. But he hated disappointing Carly, especially after he had told her they would have dinner together.

They walked together to the elevator, where they parted company. As the door closed on her elevator, Dev's cell phone rang.

"He's gone again," Lloyd said when Dev answered.

Dev was astounded that J.R. had managed to slip past the best security team in Shreveport a second time. There wasn't much he could do. He knew his men were doing the best they could.

"We'll get him next time," he told Lloyd. He shut off his phone and returned to his private office, where he walked to the window and looked out at the familiar view. But it was Carly he was thinking of, not business or the city spread out below and off into the distance.

Would they get J.R. the next time? He was proving more slippery than Dev had imagined. And Carly was clearly afraid of facing him. Dev couldn't blame her.

She had fallen for J.R.'s smooth talk once, and according to her mother he was still trying. Hadn't he realized that the Albrights had no money? It was possible that he hadn't. And possible that he had people breathing down his back about gambling debts. Hadn't Chace mentioned something similar when J.R. had caused trouble and then disappeared a few years ago?

But Dev was concerned about Carly. He had put her in a position where she might have to deal with J.R. before she was ready and sure of herself. He couldn't let that happen, and he needed a solution.

Later that night, while going over the paperwork needed for the Devil's Den's transfer of ownership, someone knocked on his door. Glancing at his watch, Dev noticed he had missed rounds, and it was later than he thought.

"You're not going to like this," Lloyd said when Dev opened the door and let him in.

Greg walked in behind Lloyd, smiling. "Maybe it isn't that bad. It could solve some problems."

Dev took the folder from Lloyd and spread the papers on his desk. After several minutes of looking through them, he found what they were talking about.

"I'll be damned." He looked up at the two men. "James Robert Staton, better known as Isle of Enve Enterprises, has the highest bid."

"It's a good thing you checked out the bidders," Greg said.

Dev smiled. "It's another of his dummy corporations, that's all. And not the first time he's used one."

When the two men had gone and he had made rounds, Dev sat at his desk. Behind him, the drapes were open to let in the first rays of the rising sun, but his thoughts were on his next step. As soon as Shirley arrived, he would have her call Norbert Jenkins with the news of his highest bid. Or highest acceptable bid, he corrected. Letters would be sent to the other bidders, apprising them of the results and the new buyer. But his plan had taken on a new twist when he met Carly.

He had spent most of the hours since he'd learned about J.R.'s bogus bid trying to make decisions about his future. He had vowed that once J.R. was behind bars he would go to the Triple B and talk to his brothers. But catching J.R. was no longer his highest priority. Carly was.

She'd come to mean more to him than he had imagined. His decision to use her to lure J.R. to the Devil's Den had been made on the spur of the moment, and now it was his responsibility to keep her safe.

He wondered how J.R. would react to the news when he received the letter with the sale announcement in it. Even a dummy corporation often had a few backers, especially when J.R. was behind it, making him possibly even more desperate to convince Carly to go ahead with the wedding, gaining him the money he needed—money he didn't know was nonexistent. Dev knew she would be better off if she were away from Shreveport and the Devil's Den, out of J.R.'s crooked, scheming way. Once he learned about the sale, J.R. might be more dangerous than Dev had imagined. As far as he knew, the man had never resorted to physical violence, but he could soon be cornered with nowhere to turn. And a cornered animal was not to be trusted. But Carly would be safe at the ranch, and he could return to Shreveport to deal with J.R. once he had her safely at the Triple B. Catching J.R. could wait a few days. Carly was more important.

After a night of sleep interrupted by strange dreams, and a quick breakfast with Dev, Carly was feeling like a long-tailed cat in a roomful of rocking chairs. She couldn't be falling in love with Dev. She just couldn't. She had no doubt that he was a good man. Everyone she talked to said the same nice things about him. A man who treated his employees the way Dev did couldn't be a man who would play devious games, as James had, or hurt anyone unnecessarily. But to be foolish enough to fall in love with him? She couldn't let herself do that.

But if it was, by some flaw in her personality, too late, she would have to leave Dev and the Devil's Den. Unfortunately she had nowhere to go and no way to get there, if she did.

Sighing, she turned the corner in the hallway and found herself at the door of the office. Hoping Shirley wouldn't be too busy to talk and provide a much-needed distraction, she turned the knob and stepped into one room.

Shirley's desk was vacant. She noticed the door to the conference room, where Dev had been the day before, and crossed to it. But, like the office, it was empty, too. Curious about the other unmarked doors, she opened another. Inside, she found a plush and ex-quisitely decorated office. But no one was sitting at the desk, and the room was empty.

Wishing she had someone—anyone—to talk to, she walked to the far corner of the outer office and stared at the only door she hadn't tried. There were no voices or sounds coming from inside, as she turned the handle and opened the door to find another dark, empty room. But as her vision quickly adjusted, she realized the room wasn't completely dark.

"Hello, there."

She jumped and turned toward the voice.

"You're Carly."

"Y-yes."

"Hey, I'm sorry if I scared you."

And then she could see him, sitting in a high-backed desk chair. In front of him were long rows of television monitors, stretching the length of the narrow room. "Is that the casino?" she asked, pointing at the screens.

"Mostly," he answered. "And other places in the hotel."

She nodded as she stared at the moving pictures before her. Of course! This was some sort of security for the casino, where the gamblers and guests were watched. "Do you catch cheaters?" she asked, her attention still glued to the screens.

"Sometimes," he answered with a chuckle. "At least, we hope we can."

"It's fascinating." And from here, she could enjoy the excitement without actually going into the casino.

"There's a chair to your right, if you'd like to sit down," he said.

Carly looked at the chair she had almost stumbled over in the dark. "So there is," she said with a little laugh. "I didn't realize this room was here."

"It's not a place the general public usually sees," he

answered, "or even thinks about. By the way, I'm Greg."

Leaning closer, she looked at him. "Oh! You were in the room yesterday when—"

"When you came to tell Dev that you'd seen J.R.?" he finished.

She nodded and noticed that he called Dev by his given name, unlike most everyone else, who called him Mr. Brannigan. "I suppose it was silly to come bursting in like that," she said, feeling foolish for being so frightened.

Shrugging, he turned back to watch the monitors. "Not really."

She wondered how much he knew about James and how she had come to be at the Devil's Den. But she was more curious about Dev. "How long have you worked for him?" she asked.

"Ever since he's owned the place."

"Did you know him before that?"

His attention never left the monitors. "Yes."

She guessed that Greg probably knew Dev better than anyone, but he didn't seem very willing to talk. It didn't matter. She was always willing to ask questions. "Then you knew him from the oil business?" she guessed.

"That's right."

"Did you work the oil fields, too?"

He turned his head to look at her. "I worked security, but it was nothing like this. Dev and I knew each other fairly well back then, and he asked if I'd come along with him to oversee security." He smiled before turning his attention back to his work. "I haven't regretted it."

Carly had a million questions to ask. What was Dev like back then? Did Greg know Dev's family? Was there something about James that she should know? Even more important, was there something about Dev that she should know? She knew so little about him. If she could learn more, she might be able to make a decision about whether she should leave or stay at the hotel.

"This is a beautiful city," she said, changing the subject to something more innocent. "Not that I've seen a lot of it. Are you from Shreveport?"

"My wife and I live across the river in Bossier."

"How long have you been married?"

"A little over a year."

"Any kids?"

He shook his head. "Not yet. She's a blackjack dealer at another casino, and we're saving up to buy a house before we start a family."

"That's smart," she replied. She was silent for a few moments before asking the next question. "Are you always here by yourself?"

"Not always. When it's busier on the floor, there are others in here. It can take more than one pair of eyes, some nights. But when it's slow, it's just me, and sometimes—"

"Hey, Greg, have you heard anything from—"

Carly spun around in the chair and saw Dev in the doorway. "Hi," she greeted.

Dev gritted his teeth and counted to ten. The Security Office was off-limits to anyone but security personnel. He was surprised Greg had allowed her inside, but he knew it was his own fault for not making a point to tell him so.

"Carly," he managed to say.

"I was just getting to know Greg," she said, giving the young man a friendly smile. She turned back to look at Dev. "This is really fascinating. Almost like being in the casino, but much safer."

Dev didn't completely agree. There was a lot happening on the floor that most people didn't see—the reason for closed-circuit cameras. Some gamblers tended to cheat. Or try to. Luckily for Dev, they were usually identified via the monitors and quickly dealt with in a way that made no one the wiser.

"Maybe you can come back later." He reached down and helped her to her feet. "Thanks for keeping her company," he told Greg.

As they were walking out the door, she looked up at him. "Then I *can* come back later?"

"Actually, no."

"But—"

"No arguments, Carly." He nodded to Shirley, sitting at her desk, and steered Carly to the door to his private office. "Stay right here. I need to get something," he said, opening the door.

"Oh, I've already been in there."

Shaking his head in exasperation, he walked in and closed the door behind him. "That's what you get for giving her the run of the place," he muttered to himself. But soon that wouldn't be a problem. She would be at the Triple B. No matter what happened with his brothers, he hoped they would find a job for her and allow her to stay. Her bubbly, friendly personality would be an asset.

He opened the tall cabinet behind his desk and took out a small box of items to put in the safe in his suite. He also grabbed several movies he had purchased, hoping Carly would like them, and tossed them into the box.

"All finished," he said, stepping out of the office with the box under his arm.

Carly joined him as he walked through the reception area. Standing on tiptoe, she tried to peek into the box. "What's in there?"

"Just some personal things I need to put away. And something for you."

"Really?"

She tried to get another look at the contents, but Dev moved the box so she couldn't. "When we get to the suite, I'll give them to you."

"Them?"

He laughed at her curiosity. "Stop fishing, Carly. You'll have to wait until we get upstairs."

"If you say so." Her pout would have been annoying if it hadn't been so adorable. And the twinkle in her eyes gave her away.

They continued down the hallway and waited at the elevator in silence. But once the car arrived and the doors closed on them, shutting them off from the world, Carly began to chatter.

"Greg is very nice," she said, staring at the ceiling. "He told me that his wife is a blackjack dealer and they're saving for a house."

"So he's told me."

"Do you know his wife?"

"Yes, I introduced them."

She looked straight at him. "You did? That's so sweet."

He smiled and shrugged, then avoided her gaze. He wasn't about to tell her that he had introduced the two only to ensure that Greg wouldn't get some crazy notion to join an offshore drilling team or take off for Alaska. He counted on Greg, who was the best head of security in all of Shreveport.

"Does his wife visit him in that room?"

He jerked around to look at her. Her air of innocence seemed genuine, but he suspected he knew exactly where this was headed. "No, she doesn't. The Security Office is for security personnel only, Carly. It's a very strict rule that we adhere to quite closely."

Her eyes widened. "Oh, dear. Does this mean Greg will lose his job for letting me stay in there? Even if it was only a few minutes?" she added.

The elevator came to a stop and they stepped out into the quiet hallway when the doors opened. "Greg isn't going to lose his job," he assured her as he keyed the lock on the door to the suite.

She slipped past him and into the sitting room. "Well, that's good to know." She gave a relieved sigh. "But there really wasn't anything in there I could see that would cause a problem. And since I've been in there once—"

"No." He set the box on the coffee table and turned to her. "Rules are rules." Holding up his hand when she started to argue, he resolved to remain stern, in spite of the look on her face that made him feel like a jerk. "Don't say it. Just because I own the place, it doesn't mean I can break the rules."

"I have a good reason."

Hoping that ignoring her would put a stop to the conversation, he changed the subject. "I bought some movies I thought you might like," he said, pointing to the box.

"Thank you," she said in a small, quiet voice. She took a deep breath and looked at him. "What I really want is a chance to become an employee. I've been learning about the hotel and its operations, and I think I can do just about anything. You probably won't let me work in the casino, but there are so many other things I could do."

He felt lower than a jerk, and the yearning in her eyes caused a large knot to form in his gut. If *his* future was iffy, hers was even more so.

Taking a few steps to reach her, he pulled her into his arms, knowing he was in for trouble but not caring. "I'd hire you in a minute, Carly. If I could."

She tipped her head back and looked up at him, her eyes filled with confusion. "But you can. You own—"

"I can't." He hated being so blunt, but he had no choice.

"But—" The word hung between them like a wall.

He didn't want to see her hurting, especially because of him. And she was. It was plain. Too plain. When she tried to pull away, he held tight, in spite of knowing that he, too, would hurt, just by being near her. His only hope was to ease the pain by telling her the truth. Or part of the truth, at least.

"I *would* hire you, Carly. You'd be an asset to the Devil's Den."

The puzzlement didn't disappear from her eyes.

"Then why don't you just do it? I promise I'd stay out of trouble. I wouldn't go near the casino or the Security—"

"I'm selling the Devil's Den."

"—Office…" Her voice trailed away as she stared at him. "Selling?"

"Yes. In fact, the papers are being drawn up now for the new owner to sign."

"But why? You're making money, right?" She waited for him to answer, and he nodded. "Then why would you sell a money-making business? Unless you didn't like the business. Is that it? You don't like the hotel casino business?"

"It's not that," he answered, wanting to put just a little distance between them. Touching her, holding her, was the worst kind of torture, when he knew he couldn't do anymore. It would be taking advantage of her, and he had done enough of that. He would never forgive himself, not when his future was so uncertain. She deserved more.

"The truth is I never intended to keep the place forever," he explained. "I proved what I set out to do when I won the poker game. I took a run-down piece of property that didn't even make enough to pay the taxes, and I turned it into one of the most popular and profitable places in the area."

"So the fun's over? Is that it?"

"No, it isn't. It's a business move that's been in the works for a long time."

"Oh." She shook her head, as if trying to make sense of what he was telling her.

"I'm working on an idea for a job for you," he

said, hoping it would cheer her up. "If that's what you really want."

"Yes," she answered slowly. "Yes, of course it is."

But he could see her indecision and feel it in her body. It was his fault. He had taken her from that church with very little thought for her, except that she was in distress because of a man who had been his enemy for years. But if he hadn't been there, what would she have done? Gone home? Waited for family and friends to comfort her, and then… Then what? Let J.R. talk her into going ahead with the wedding?

"Carly," he began, but didn't know what to say to make things right. Her innocent vulnerability clawed at his insides, while it heated his blood to the point of a rolling boil. He cared about her. He wanted her. He wanted—

His self-control gone, he lowered his head to capture her lips with his, while his head buzzed and his body throbbed with need.

"There's someone at the door," she whispered.

Her lips were so close, he felt her breath brush his own lips, nearly driving him over the edge.

The door?

The buzzing continued, and as he realized what it was, he let go of her. Reluctantly. Turning, he walked to the door, not completely aware of what he was doing, and opened it.

"Phone call in the office for you, boss," Lloyd said.

Dev blinked once but didn't speak.

Lloyd looked past him to Carly and back again. "I think you'll want to take this in private," he said in a low voice.

"Yes. Okay," Dev answered, his head beginning to clear. "I'll be right there." Closing the door when Lloyd moved to leave, he turned back to Carly. "I have to go take care of this, but I'll be back. And I'll explain everything."

For a long moment she didn't speak or move, but she finally nodded.

He hurried from the suite, eager to get the call over with and get back to Carly. He couldn't imagine who or what would make the call so important. Or so private.

"This is Brannigan."

"Hello, Dev."

As soon as he heard the voice on the other end of the line, the muscles in his jaw tightened. "Jimmy Bob Staton. I've been expecting to hear from you."

J.R. laughed. "I figured you'd find out about that corporation, but it was worth a try."

"I'm a better businessman than to let something like that slip by me, J.R. You should know that."

For a moment the line was silent. "I didn't call about the sale of the Devil's Den."

Dev's hand tightened on the receiver. Turning in his chair, he faced the broad window overlooking the city. "No?" he asked, knowing full well why the weasel had called.

"I just finished speaking with Carly's mother in Baton Rouge," J.R. said in a concerned tone of voice. "She's very worried about her little girl."

"Who?"

"Come on, Brannigan. I know she's there."

"And you know this how?" Dev was certain he

didn't have any proof Carly was there, and he wasn't going to tell him she was.

"Stop asking questions and answer mine," J.R. demanded.

Dev smiled at the hint of frustration in the man's voice. "You haven't asked any."

"Then it's time I do. Where is she?"

"This is getting tedious. She who?"

"You know damned well who I'm talking about," J.R. answered. "I saw you leave the church with her and saw her in your car."

"It's a Jeep," Dev answered, goading him.

"Whatever. She was with you. I promised her mother that I'd bring her home."

Dev nearly laughed at J.R.'s attempt at bluffing. If Carly's mother had truly wanted her daughter home, Carly would be there now. All she had to do was tell him she wanted or needed to go home, and he would drop everything to get her there. Even though he didn't want to think about her leaving.

"I can't help you, J.R.," he said, honestly.

"Sure you can. Give Carly my number and tell her that her mother wants her home," J.R. replied. "That's all you have to do. I'll take it from there."

Dev had known J.R. long enough to recognize his little tricks, and he wasn't dumb enough to fall for this one. If he didn't know better, he would think J.R. wasn't playing with a full deck. Any gambler worth his weight in chips played his cards close to his chest. J.R.'s finesse—if he had ever possessed any—was slipping. No wonder he owed a fortune in gambling debts. It was possible that the man's sudden lack of smarts was due to the pressure he was probably under to pay off those debts, which also accounted for his need for Carly.

Dev wasn't falling for it. "You're welcome to come check the place yourself," he offered, taking a gamble. If J.R. took him up on it, the Feds would be there faster than ol' James Robert Staton could deal a hand.

But Carly wouldn't be anywhere near when J.R.'s fall came down. He wouldn't put her in that position. Not now. Not when he was close to getting her away from Shreveport and any more grief J.R. could cause her.

"I—" J.R. cleared his throat. "I'm not able to, at this time. Just pass along the message."

Before Dev could respond, the line went dead. He wasn't sure what to think. J.R. might still be trying to bluff and hoping security at the Devil's Den would weaken if Dev thought Carly was safe. "I'm not that dumb, either, you weasel," he announced to his empty office.

After a quick call to Greg about strengthening security, he felt better. In a matter of days Carly would be safe in Texas at the Triple B. J.R. wouldn't have the guts to show up there.

Reminded that he needed to call his brothers to make sure a visit would be welcome and they wouldn't mind if he brought along a guest, Dev dialed the number for the Triple B and counted the rings, eager to get things moving. Carly's future was at stake. And eventually his, too, especially when he told his brothers that he had killed their father.

Chapter Eight

Bored, Carly paced the sitting room of the suite, wishing Dev would return to take up where they left off. Just the thought of him almost kissing her only to be called away had her so frustrated she couldn't be still.

She glanced at her watch again. It had been over twenty minutes since he had hurried out the door. If he wasn't interested in kissing her, she could at least ask more questions. He must have gone mad to even think of selling the Devil's Den.

And what was he going to do, with no business, no home, no…nothing? She knew what it felt like to have nothing, and she wouldn't wish it on anybody, especially not on him. If the place was as bad as he said it was when he won it, he had to have worked hard and spent a lot of money to get it to the height of popularity that it was now. Most people wouldn't have bothered.

Didn't he worry about his employees? She had hoped to be one of them. They liked him so much, it wasn't fair to do this to them. It wasn't fair to do this to *her*.

Sinking to the sofa, she propped her chin in her hands. She had so hoped that she could talk him into hiring her. Even if she had the nerve to apply at another casino, without experience she doubted anyone else would hire her. Or maybe that's what he meant by working on a possible job for her.

But even that thought didn't cheer her. She wanted to work for Dev. She wanted to be near him, to see him every day. And she knew that wouldn't happen if she worked somewhere else.

It was foolish to want those things, but she couldn't stop herself. Just seeing him sent her heart racing, and the thought of being kissed again—

Giving herself a shake, she was determined not to think about that. It led to flights of fancy, as her mother would say. Bless her mother, who was prone to those sorts of things herself.

She sighed and leaned back, spotting the box he had brought from the office on the table in front of her. A movie would take her mind off Dev, she decided. Leaning forward, she read the titles, hoping something would catch her interest enough to distract her until he came back. One tape was different from the others, and when she picked it up, her eyes widened. Instead of a movie title, she saw her name hand-printed in heavy block letters.

"This is strange," she said, standing and crossing to the entertainment system. She slipped it into the machine and pressed the button to start it, waiting for a picture of who knew what.

Seconds later she saw herself on the screen, a little distorted, but definitely her. And she continued to see herself, here, there and everywhere. Of course. The security cameras. But why a tape of her?

So engrossed in the images of herself that she didn't hear the door open, she was startled when she heard Dev's voice.

"Everything is taken care of," he said, walking toward her.

He was grinning as he slipped out of his suit jacket and tossed it to the sofa, but she was too stunned to react. Normally there was no way to fend off that sexy grin. But she was having a problem grasping what she had seen—and was still seeing—on the screen.

His gaze shifted from her to the television, and his smile was instantly replaced by a frown. "Where did you get that?"

Her mind cleared enough for a reaction to set in, complete with questions vying to be asked and answered. "I think a better question would be, where did it come from and why do you have it?"

He walked to the entertainment center and reached out to the VCR, shutting it off. As he turned around, he tugged at the patch over his eye. "I can explain."

She waited while he stood looking at her yet not really looking at her. "And?"

"They're clips from the security tapes," he finally said.

"Even I figured that one out." The thought crossed her mind that she might have figured him wrong. But she couldn't have. He just wasn't the type to watch from a distance, like a Peeping Tom.

"I'm selling the hotel."

Exasperated with herself and him, she blew out a breath of air. "We covered that earlier."

"I guess I do owe you an explanation," he said, moving across the room, away from her.

"It is kind of...weird."

He turned to look at her and tugged at the patch again. "I had the clips removed to ensure your privacy. Let's face it, Carly, the new owner might wonder at seeing you everywhere," he explained. "The rest of the staff will still be here, but you'll be missing. No sense in leaving questions in the new owner's mind. He might wonder what had happened to you. And to be honest, I wasn't comfortable with leaving them in. For your sake."

The only answer she had was "Oh."

She felt like a fool for thinking there might be some other reason. Of course he wasn't the stalker type. Why would he need to do something like that? Mercy sakes, she lived right in the same suite he did. He could watch her anytime.

Removing the clips was a very noble act. He had saved her from, well, from nothing that would really harm her, but the fact was that he had been thinking of her. He had been so—

Disappointment flooded her, and the rush she had felt only a few moments before disappeared. There was no other word for it. And it was totally unromantic. He was being kind, nothing more. Something a big brother might do for his little sister. Just looking out for her best interest. How utterly depressing!

She didn't want him to see the sudden blue funk she had fallen into. A long, silent cry in the bedroom would be the perfect thing to do. Patting his arm in a sisterly way, she thanked him and tried not to sniff. Tears were already threatening.

Dev put his hand over hers, wishing he had remembered to take out the movies and put away the box. He couldn't believe he had been so distracted by her earlier that he'd forgotten to remove the tape of her. He couldn't tell her the truth—that he had saved the clips to remember her by. His future was still unsure. Too unsure to plan anything more than getting to the ranch, nabbing J.R. and admitting to his brothers that their father's heart attack had been his fault. He was trying to handle too much at once. And he was doing a poor job with everything. Not his normal operating standard.

"We need to talk," he said, before she could slip away.

She looked up at him, disappointment clouding her eyes. "I thought we just did."

Her gaze held him frozen in the moment. He had certainly managed to botch a conversation that hadn't needed to take place. "About your future," he said, hoping she would at least give him a chance.

A spark of anger flashed in her eyes. "What about yours?" she asked. "Do *you* have a future? And what about your employees?"

"My employees will be taken care of."

"How can you be sure of that?"

Dev didn't see what this had to do with Carly or

her future, or even his, but she deserved some sort of explanation. "For one thing, I made sure they would still have jobs after the sale. For another, I'll personally help anyone who loses their job, as long as it wasn't for something I would have fired them for myself."

Her expression softened. "I should've known you would do something like that and had it all covered. But what about you? Do you have plans?"

How could he tell her what his plans involved? Especially when his plans depended on his brothers' reaction to the news that he was responsible for their father's death.

"Why don't we sit down?" he suggested, guiding her to the sofa. He sat next to her, close enough to enjoy her nearness but not so close that he felt he would lose control. When they were both settled comfortably, he took a deep breath and focused on her.

"I have plans to visit my brothers at our ranch in Texas," he explained. "I need to leave as soon as possible."

Her grin was infectious. "See? I was right."

"About what?"

"I knew you were from Texas," she said, with a know-it-all smile of satisfaction.

"Yes, you were," he admitted, chuckling. "But I haven't lived there since—well, for a long time. Would you like to go with me?" He waited, hoping she would say yes.

Her smile disappeared, and her eyes widened. "You're serious, aren't you?"

"Of course I am. There might be a job there for you,

if you're interested," he added. "It's not a sure thing. I haven't talked to my brothers about it yet, but I'm hopeful."

"I don't know anything about ranching."

Reaching out, he took her hand. "It's not just a regular ranch. The Triple B is a working dude ranch. Has been for the past three years, since my youngest brother, Trey, talked Chace and me into letting him turn it into one. From what they've told me, business is booming, so on top of the regular ranching, there are a lot of guests to see to. It would be similar enough to a hotel that you might enjoy it."

Her eyes brightened again. "I think I would."

Dev hoped so. And once that was taken care of, he would return to the Devil's Den, wrap up the sale and put J.R. behind bars where he belonged. But Carly didn't need to know that. Not now. Maybe never. Definitely not before he talked to his brothers.

But whatever happened, when the time came, he owed her an explanation. And an apology.

"Tell me about the ranch," she said.

He didn't answer immediately. His future loomed before him and, although it might be uncertain, he didn't doubt it would be unsuccessful, whether he was welcomed home by his brothers or not.

"It's in the Hill Country, northwest of San Antonio," he said as images of his home jumped into his mind. His visits to the ranch had been few and far between and only for short periods of time. But he hadn't forgotten even the tiniest detail of the Triple B. "Some folks call it the Banderas, and there's a town in the area called Bandera."

"Sounds like something from an old Western movie."

"A place where the *bandidos* would hide?" he asked with a chuckle. "That's a good description. It's rough country. Rocky. Not much good for farming, but great ranching. And the sunsets…" He closed his eyes and savored the memory. "Every color of the rainbow, and the fields are full of wildflowers in the spring and early summer."

Carly sighed and turned to lean back against him. "It sounds beautiful and so different from here. What about the ranch itself? I've never been on a ranch."

He recognized a hint of uncertainty in her voice and instinctively pulled her closer, wrapping his arms around her. "Chace handles most of the ranching," he explained, hoping it would reassure her. "He has a lot of help with it. There's a bunkhouse full of hands. Has to be, with that much land and cattle to oversee."

Turning her head, she looked up at him. "How much land?"

"Somewhere around a hundred thousand acres, give or take a few."

"That much?" she gasped. "It must be half the size of Texas."

"Not even close," Dev said, laughing. "But wait until you see it."

"And the dude ranch? What about it?"

"Trey does a good job of running it. He proved that his idea was a good one, even though Chace and I thought he was crazy at first."

"So it's really possible that they might want to hire me?"

Dev slipped his fingers around a lock of her copper-colored hair, and a lump formed in his throat at the note of hope in her voice. "Very possible," he whispered close to her ear.

"I can't even imagine," Carly whispered in return. "I hope they like me."

Gently turning her to face him, he lost himself in her eyes. "How could they not?"

"Well," she answered, the corners of her mouth turning down, "it sounds like a family thing."

He nodded, still entranced. "It is. Chace and Dev are both married now. They all live in the ranch house, but I heard that Chace and Ellie are starting to build a new house nearby. But what difference does that make?"

"Sometimes families don't like people who…well, who intrude."

"And you think you'd be an intruder?" he asked.

She shrugged. "Maybe."

"You could never be an intruder," he whispered as he began to kiss his way up her neck. Her skin was velvety smooth and hot, emboldening him to do more.

When he reached her ear, he nibbled and felt her shiver. "Will you go with me?" he asked again.

"If you want me to," she answered on a sigh.

He leaned back, putting only inches between them. Her eyes were dark with need, carrying him beyond the boundaries he knew he shouldn't cross. "What do you think I want?"

"I'm not sure," she whispered.

"Then I'll show you."

He took his time, until his lips touched hers. Seduction was an art. But this wasn't seduction, it was… He wasn't sure what it was as he brushed her lips with his, teasing her to open for him. When she did, his control vanished.

Carly's moan of pleasure came from the tip of her toes and rippled upward through her body until it escaped her lips. This was what she had been craving for days—the feel of Dev's hands on her back, his mouth pressed to hers. She didn't want it to end.

As he kissed his way slowly and deliciously up her neck again, the thought drifted through her mind that her mother would find it shameful. It *was* wanton, but she didn't care. She'd been good all her life. It was time to be bad, especially if bad felt so good.

Moving slightly, she touched the top button of his shirt and slipped it through the buttonhole. The act felt so brazen and gave her such pleasure that she continued with the next one.

"What are you doing?" Dev asked softly as he nibbled her earlobe.

"Mmm," was her only reply as she continued to the last button. When she had eased the last button open, she spread the shirt wide and traced her finger down the center of his chest, eliciting a shiver from him. Smiling at the power it gave her, she looked up to see him looking at her, his eyes dark with desire. It was all she needed to continue. Oh, yes, she had the desire, but this was new territory for her. Sharing kisses with men wasn't completely new, but she had never been given the opportunity to explore a man's body as Dev was now allowing her.

While their gazes remained locked, she splayed her hands wide across his muscled chest and felt his strength.

"Carly…" His husky voice held a note of uncertainty.

She ignored him. She wasn't going to stop. She couldn't. Pressing her lips to his chest, she felt his heart pounding beneath them. Her hand slipped to the button of his black pants, and her fingers fumbled at it.

"Carly," he said, his voice strained, "we can't do this."

She looked into his eyes, determined that he wouldn't stop her. "Yes, we can."

"Think about it, Carly."

She sat up, straddling him, and reached for the hem of her top to pull it over her head. "I have."

He reached for her hands and stilled them. "Then think again. Please."

She relaxed her hold on her top and took a deep breath. "Is it because I'm…inexperienced?"

He gently pulled her hands away and pressed kisses into her palms. "No."

"Then what?"

Pulling her back to rest against him, he held her. "A lot of things. But not that."

Deep in her heart she knew he was right. But she didn't want to admit it.

"Things are too uncertain," he continued. "Even with the plans I've made, my future isn't stable. Not yet. And yours is even less so."

"But—"

He pressed a finger to her lips. "Trust me on this, Carly."

She shook her head, not wanting to listen. "I don't care about plans. I care about now. Here. Us."

"So do I," he said softly, and brushed her hair away from her face. "But this isn't the right time."

She was silent for a moment, studying his face. "This isn't easy for you, is it?" she asked.

His laugh held no humor. "Not at all. In fact, it's a bit…uncomfortable," he admitted with a sexy grin. She started to pull away, but he held her tight. "I can handle it. But what I want you to understand—and I know it'll make you mad to hear it—is that it's for your own good. If something did happen—this happened— I wouldn't want you regretting it tomorrow or next week or even years from now. I don't want to risk that. Being a little, uh, uncomfortable isn't worth it."

She wanted to get mad but she couldn't. He was being honest, and she should be, too. "You're right," she admitted. "I'm sorry."

"No sorrier than I am. I started this, not you."

She leaned close and kissed him. "We both did."

His answer was a smile, and then he moved her and sat up. "It's getting late, and I need to start rounds."

"When will we leave for the ranch?" she asked, straightening her top and smoothing her hair with her fingers.

"I'll make the reservations immediately for the first flight in the morning." He stood and turned to look at her.

"That soon?" she asked, surprised.

Reaching out, he took her hands and helped her up, then he pulled her close. "The sooner we get there, the sooner we'll know if you have a job. That's what you want, isn't it?"

She nodded but felt a little uncertain. She didn't

know his family. They were strangers. But she trusted him.

He let go of her and picked up his suit jacket. He slipped it on as he headed for the door, but he turned around when he reached for the handle. "You might want to let your mother know where you'll be."

"I'll call her later, after I've packed."

"Does she have the number here?"

"No, I never gave it to her."

He let go of the door handle and stepped away from the door. "Why not?"

She shrugged, feeling bad that she had kept her whereabouts a secret from her mother. "I wanted to be on my own. On my own terms. If she'd had the number…"

"I think I understand," he said. He reached into his jacket and pulled out a small pad of paper and a pen. "This is the number for the ranch," he said as he scribbled on the paper. "I'd feel better if you gave it to her."

She walked over to him and took it. "You're right. Again. Thank you."

Cupping her cheek in his hand, he leaned down to brush his lips across hers. "It's going to be a busy night. I have a lot to get done before we can leave, so I probably won't see you until early in the morning."

"I'll have everything packed," she told him. "Not that I have that much to pack."

He kissed her again before he slipped out. She closed the door behind him and leaned against it. Taking a deep breath and letting it out slowly, she silently prayed that she had made the right decision about going to the ranch.

Chapter Nine

Dev walked into the ranch's big kitchen to find Carly helping his two sisters-in-law clear the kitchen table after the midday dinner. As he had expected, his family had greeted her with open arms and no questions, and Carly was fitting right in with them.

"You might want to take a jacket," Ellie told her.

Dev winked at Carly and grinned at his older brother's wife. "In case you haven't noticed, it's pretty warm out there."

Ellie laughed and placed her hand on her rounded belly. "You're right. I keep thinking that because I'm warmer than normal, everyone else must be cold." She turned to Carly. "Don't listen to me," she said, putting an arm around her. "Pregnancy is making me overly motherly. You and Dev go on with your ride and don't worry about these dishes. Meg and I can finish up when she gets back from the guests' lunch."

"But I really don't—"

"You're a guest," Ellie said. She gave Carly a gentle push toward Dev, who caught her hand and tugged her in the direction of the door. "Plenty of time to be one of the family."

Dev caught the strange look Ellie shot him before ducking out the door with Carly. He hoped his sister-in-law wasn't expecting Carly to become a member of the Brannigan family. Although the idea wasn't a bad one, all he hoped for now was that his brothers would agree to hire her.

Still holding Carly's hand, he gave it a squeeze as they stepped out onto the wide porch that wrapped around three sides of the big house. "I told you they'd like you."

She looked up and smiled at him. "And I like them. A lot. You're very lucky to have such a wonderful family."

Dev nodded but was silent, realizing again that in some ways he had been a fool to want to leave the Triple B when he was young. But that's what he had chosen to do and, in general, his life since then had been good. He'd been lucky. But along with the good things had been the guilt he carried. And he still had to deal with that. Soon. Very soon.

After saddling two horses, they rode out to the far pasture. "I spent a lot of time out here when I was a kid," Dev told her as they dismounted. "A lot of time thinking."

Carly was quiet as they both gazed out at the beauty of one of the creeks that ran through parts of the Brannigan spread. "I can see why. It's so beautiful. So peaceful."

"It was a long time ago." But standing there, he was flooded with memories. On his trips back home, he hadn't come down to this particular spot. He'd had a feeling what would happen if he did. He'd been right.

Pulling her into his arms, he put the past to rest for at least a while. "Now that you've met my family, do you think you might be happy here?" he asked, hoping for a positive response.

"Definitely," she answered. "The ranch is beautiful and so different from Louisiana. I'm looking forward to the change."

"That's good," he said, leaning down to steal a kiss. "But I want you to be sure, before I talk to my brothers about it."

Her eyes sparkled. "I am sure. How could I not be? Your family is wonderful. I only hope they feel the same and can find me a position."

"What about your mother?" he asked. "It's a lot farther from here to Baton Rouge than it was from Shreveport. Not that you wouldn't be able to visit now and then."

She shook her head, and the sunlight danced in her hair as it moved, setting it on fire. "I don't have any reason to go back that often. Mama will be well taken care of. I'm sure of it."

"You're sure?"

Tilting her head to the side, she looked at him. "Are you trying to talk me out of staying?"

"No," he said, pulling her closer. "I only want to be sure it's what you want."

"It is," she said, nodding. "I love it here already."

Vowing that he wouldn't let himself get carried away, he pressed his lips to hers. She tasted of sunlight and outdoors, and when she reached up to wind her arms around his neck, his resolve nearly vanished. He held on to his control, unable to end the kiss but knowing he had to before it went any further.

"We need to head back," he whispered against her lips. He was eager to talk to his brothers and hoped he would have good news for her soon.

"I suppose you're right," she answered with a sigh and pulled away to step back. Together they walked to where they'd left the horses grazing, and Dev helped her mount. "Can we come out here again?" she asked as he mounted his own horse.

"Someday." At least he hoped they would. He didn't know if his home would be at the ranch.

The ride back to the ranch house went quickly, and Dev left Carly with his sisters-in-law, while he went in search of his brothers. He found Chace coming in from the barn, and together they found Trey in the ranch office.

Stepping inside the room was like a trip back into the past, and Dev felt like hightailing it right back out the door. The office had been his father's domain, where business was done over imported cigars and glasses of expensive bourbon. It was also where punishment had been administered for any and all infractions of the rules. Leather furniture, softened with age, sat in the same places where it had sixteen years earlier, as did the big, scarred oak desk that dominated the room. On one wall, a portrait of their grandfather, Buford Brannigan, looked down on them. On another wall a large map of the ranch stretched from window frame to window frame. It had been and still was a man's room.

But it was Trey, not Buck Brannigan, who sat behind the desk now, with his feet propped on the top as he leaned back in the high-backed leather desk chair. "Get a glass, Dev," he told his brother, holding up a bottle, "and one for Chace. I feel a celebration coming on."

Dev walked to the small table in the corner and picked up two heavy tumblers. "Don't jump to conclusions, baby brother," he said, moving to the desk. "There's nothing to celebrate."

Trey moved his feet to the floor and leaned across the desk to fill the glasses. "You showed up with a pretty lady. And a nice one, at that. I'd say that's cause for celebration. Wouldn't you, Chace?"

Sitting in one of the wing chairs, Chace took the glass Dev handed him and crossed one booted foot over his knee. "It's certainly out of the ordinary. I can't say I'm not pleased, but I am a bit surprised." His eyes narrowed as he studied Dev. "Does this mean you have an announcement to make?"

Dev shook his head. "But I have a favor to ask."

For a moment neither of his brothers spoke, and he hesitated to begin, not completely sure they would be willing to listen to him.

"What are you waiting for?" Chace asked.

"Yeah," Trey agreed. "Ask away."

Dev relaxed. He should've known his brothers wouldn't deny him. Not yet anyway. "Carly needs a job."

Trey nodded, but he didn't smile. "Okay, but what can she do? Any special skills?"

Dev thought for a minute. As far as he knew, she didn't have any office skills. He didn't even know if she could type. But he did know that she would be an asset at the Triple B. "She gets along with everybody. A people person," he finally said. "Comes from an old, prominent Baton Rouge family. You know the type. Debutantes and barbecues."

"This isn't *Gone with the Wind*, Dev," Chase said, looking at Trey.

Dev knew he wasn't giving her the glowing recommendation he had hoped he would, but it was hard to explain Carly to people who didn't know her. "I know that," he said, tugging at the patch over his eye, "but I don't know what else I can tell you, except that she's interested in everybody and everything. I doubt she's ever met a stranger."

"I don't have a problem with hiring her," Trey said, standing. He picked up his glass and walked around the desk to sit on the edge of it. "We're in need of more help. Meg's been complaining about never having any free time. We hardly see each other, except when the guests aren't around."

"And Ellie needs to take it easy," Chace chimed in. "Once the baby comes, she'll be lucky if she has time to do the exhibition riding."

"So we agree that we'll hire Carly," Trey finished. "We'd just like to know a little more about her."

Chace nodded. "Like how and where did you meet her?"

Dev did his best to contain his happiness. Carly's future was no longer a question. "Get comfortable," he told Trey. He settled into one of the empty chairs and took a deep breath. "You probably wonder what I've been doing all these years."

Trey looked at Chace and back at Dev. "Who? Us? You bet we've been wondering, but we didn't ask. It was your business."

"And that's what I've been doing," Dev said. "Business. I own the Devil's Den Casino Hotel in Shreveport."

Chace dropped his foot to the floor and leaned forward. "You're kidding."

"For the past three years," Dev answered. Taking a drink of the amber-colored liquid in his glass, he closed his eyes and leaned back. "And you'll never guess who showed up as one of the patrons."

Trey put his glass down with a thud. "J.R."

"None other," Dev said with a grin. After taking another sip, he explained how he had won the business and built it to a money-making gambling establishment. He also told them how he had learned of J.R.'s wedding in Baton Rouge.

"And that's where I met Carly, ditching her groom at the altar," he said, ending the story.

"Carly was going to marry Jimmy Bob?" Chace asked. "Are you sure…?"

"She wasn't involved with anything," Dev answered before his brother could finish the question. "J.R. was after her money. Only there isn't any. And as far as I know, he still doesn't know that. She's as trustworthy as you and I are."

"Damn," Chace said, getting to his feet. "Damn."

Trey laughed. "My sentiments exactly. Looks like she has a lot in common with Ellie, Chace."

"I figure she couldn't be anywhere safer than at the Triple B," Dev told them both.

"You're right," Chace said. "He's too much of a coward to show up here."

"But I think he figured out that she was with me at the Devil's Den," Dev added. "He didn't have any proof, and I was able to bluff, but I can't be certain. I'll head back to Shreveport tomorrow. With Carly safe here, where I won't have to worry about her running into him, I'll be able to concentrate on catching him. He steps one foot in the Den, and I'll have him arrested."

Trey gave him a brotherly slap to the back. "And come home a hero. You don't know how bad Chace and I want to see him get his just desert."

"I think I have a clue," Dev told him with a rueful smile.

"But what I want to know is exactly what's going on with you and your pretty lady," Trey said, settling back behind the desk again.

It wasn't a question Dev was willing to answer. He still had J.R. to put behind bars. And once that was taken care of, he would come back to the Triple B to tell his brothers the truth. All of it. Until then, he couldn't commit himself. Not to Carly. Not to anything.

"I don't know how to thank you all." Carly's gaze included the entire family seated around the large but cozy living room of the ranch house. Having just learned that she had been hired as an employee, she was practically speechless.

"We should probably thank *you*," Ellie said, smiling sweetly, "and Dev, too, for bringing you to us."

Meg nodded in agreement. "Ellie and I have been

so busy, we've hardly had time to enjoy anything. Tonight has been very special. I hope there'll be more evenings like this, when we can all get together."

Helping his pregnant wife to her feet, Chace turned to the others. "It'll be great having everyone here, for a change," he said, looking pointedly at Dev.

Dev smiled, but Carly noticed that it didn't reach his eyes. She had noticed several things about him during the evening get-together. He had always been somewhat reserved about some things, but with his brothers, with whom she had thought he would be more open with, there were times when he seemed to withdraw into himself. But one thing was very clear to her. His brothers loved and respected him as much as he did them. She truly envied them all and wished that, maybe someday, she might be something more than a member of the staff.

Hope was strong in her heart, especially when she saw the look on Dev's face as he helped her from the chair where she was sitting. His eyes shone with something she was afraid to name. She hoped it was love, but she also knew she shouldn't hope too much. It would be wonderful, though, not to be disappointed this one time.

"You're tired," he said, when she covered a yawn with her hand.

"Only a little," she admitted.

They bid the others good-night, and Dev walked with her up the wide staircase that led from the entry hall. A few steps from the top, she realized she had left one of her small bags in the rental car they had driven from the airport.

"I'll be right back," she said, turning and starting down the stairs. "I left my bag in the car."

Dev followed her. "I'll go with—"

"Hey, Dev," Chace called from the living room, "come see this. You aren't going to believe it."

At the door, Dev stopped her. "If you'll wait—"

"No, it's all right," she told him, standing on tiptoe to kiss his cheek. "I know where the car is. I'll only be a minute. Go see what Chace wants."

He smiled and nodded, then joined his brother in the living room.

Slipping out the door and onto the porch, Carly breathed deeply. The smells were definitely different from the ones she was accustomed to, but she couldn't say she didn't like them. The ranch was a whole new world for her. A new life. And she was determined to make it the best she could.

As she walked across the yard in the dark to the parked rental car, she couldn't help but notice how the star-studded sky seemed to nearly wrap itself around her, promising a peace she hadn't experienced since childhood. Yes, she thought as she reached the car, she was going to love it here. And maybe, in time, Dev would—"

"Hello, Carly."

She froze. She knew the voice and had fervently hoped she would never hear it again. "What are you doing here, James?" she asked, turning to face the bridegroom she had left behind at the church.

He stepped out of the shadows and approached her. "You're looking very well, Carly."

She recognized the seductive tone of his voice, but

she wasn't going to fall for it. Her first impulse was to run, but running for the house wouldn't put an end to it, so she decided to stay and hear him out. Not that she would ever again believe a word he said.

"I'm feeling very rested, thank you." Taking a step back, she bumped against the side of the car. She wasn't frightened. At least not much. "What are you doing here?"

"Yes, it's very restful here," he said, as if he hadn't heard her question. He looked around, peering into the darkness. "Trey has done a lot with the place."

"So, you do know them."

"Very well, as a matter of fact. My family's ranch is just over that ridge." He pointed into the darkness. "What's left of it, anyway," he added, more to himself than to her.

"You haven't answered my question. Why are you here?"

Turning back to her, he smiled. "I've come to take you home."

Realizing he had no control over her and never had, she was no longer frightened. "And if I don't want to go?" she asked, feeling more sure than ever that he wouldn't harm her.

"Your mother asked me to find you," he explained. "She's been very worried. I know you don't want to disappoint her. You were confused and frightened, that's all, and I understand that. It all happened so quickly. For both of us. If you'll just come with me, I'll take you home to your mother, and we'll set things right. She wants to see the wedding take place, Carly.

She wants to see us legally wed. Man and wife. Mr. and Mrs. James Robert Staton."

Before she had the chance to tell him that she would not be returning to Shreveport—with him or anyone else—and that there wouldn't be a wedding, she saw Dev coming toward them in the dark. "Something tells me Dev isn't going to let that happen," she said, unable to hide her smile.

"Nope, don't think I will," Dev said as he came to a stop beside her once-intended. "I'm surprised to see you here, Jimmy Bob."

James took a step backward. "Just being neighborly," he stammered.

"I'd stay put, if I were you," Dev said, his tone threatening. "You and I have a lot to talk about."

Squaring his shoulders, James faced him. "Then let's start with what you were doing crashing my wedding and kidnapping my bride."

Dev glanced at Carly before answering. "I think you can figure that one out for yourself. And it's a damned good thing I was there, wouldn't you say? But kidnapping? Not even close."

"I went with him freely," Carly added, as Chace and Ellie stepped out of the darkness to join them.

James shifted from one foot to the other as he looked at her. "Your mother asked me to bring you home," he stated again.

Dev laughed. "I think we all know that's bull."

"I talked to my mama on the phone yesterday, James," Carly explained. "She knows exactly where I am, so don't even try to tell me different."

Tiny Ellie stepped up to James, her hands on her

hips and her head tipped back to look at him. "I can't believe you have the nerve to show up here. What you tried to do to me was bad enough, but it's clear you didn't learn your lesson because you had to go and try it again with someone else." She walked over to Carly and slipped her arm around her waist. "Someone who is very sweet and dear to us."

Tears burned Carly's eyes. "Thank you, Ellie," she whispered.

As Ellie gave her a sisterly hug, Meg joined the group. "They're on their way."

James looked from one to the other. "They?" he asked.

Chace took his place on the other side of James. "As they say in the old movies, the jig is up, Jimmy Bob."

Carly turned her head to see red flashing lights coming up the long drive to the ranch. There was no doubt in her mind that the police were coming for James, but she wasn't completely sure why. Dev had told her that her former fiancé had been known to do some questionable things, but she hadn't realized they were bad enough that the authorities would·be interested in him.

Meg moved closer and slipped her arm around Carly, too. "Why don't we go up to the house and let the men handle things?" she suggested. "They don't need us for this. The sheriff and the others will take care of it."

The first of several official cars came to a stop near the group of family members. Ellie and Meg greeted the officers in passing as they walked with Carly up to the house.

"Are they arresting him?" Carly asked, looking back over her shoulder.

"Yes," Meg answered.

"And none too soon," Ellie added. "Carly, honey, you don't know how close you came to being ruined by that man."

The three of them stepped up onto the porch, and a shiver shook Carly as she turned to look at Ellie. "I know he was marrying me for my family's money. Dev explained that. And I know he tried to do the same to you, but for different reasons."

"Oil," Ellie said, opening the door and following the others inside the house. "He tried it with other people, too. And other scams. He just managed to disappear before anyone could catch him. He would've taken every cent your family has."

"Which isn't much," Carly said, sadly. "But he didn't know that."

"Trey told me that J.R. owes Dev a fortune in gambling expenses," Meg added. "Others, too."

"And Chace has suspected for some time that he's running from what might be the Mob." Ellie's shiver matched Carly's. "Dev has been waiting for this moment for a long time. They all have."

The three of them stopped at the foot of the staircase, and Carly looked from one woman to the other. "So this isn't something new? They've been trying to do this for a while? To catch James? Or J.R. or whoever he is?"

Ellie shrugged. "Chace and Trey have been mostly hoping he'd be caught. It seems Dev has been doing more about it than any of us knew."

"But don't worry yourself about it," Meg said, giving Carly a hug before releasing her. "You were lucky, and obviously smarter than you realized, when you walked out on him at your wedding."

Too shaken and confused to answer, Carly nodded. "I...I think I'd like to go to my room."

"I'm sure you're exhausted," Ellie said. "We'll all be up for a while yet, I'm sure, so if you need anything—"

"I will," Carly answered and started up the stairs. Stopping, she turned back to look at Ellie and Meg. "Thank you both. For everything."

"You don't need to thank us," Meg said. "Sleep well."

Carly answered with a smile and continued up the stairs to the room Ellie had shown her earlier. Her head was spinning with memories of what had occurred, but one word kept repeating itself in her mind.

Kidnapping.

She knew Dev hadn't kidnapped her, but his reason for rescuing her and taking her to the Devil's Den was becoming crystal clear.

Opening the door to her room, she walked inside and sank to the bed. What had she been thinking, hoping for things that obviously meant nothing to him? He had never mentioned a future with her. In fact, the only future they had talked about was hers, here on the ranch. She had no idea what he would do once the Devil's Den was sold, but she suspected it wouldn't be settling on the Triple B, or he would have said so. She had foolishly thought he cared for her. Once again she was wrong. Impulsive. Blind and much too trusting. To him, she was nothing more than a pawn in a plan to bring James to justice. He had used her to lure James to the Devil's Den. And that didn't make Dev much better than the man who would soon be behind bars.

Standing, Carly crossed to the window that looked out on the ranch yard. All over the ranch, lights were blazing, and it appeared that even the dude ranch guests had come out of their cabins to see what was happening. She could see Dev talking to a group of law enforcement people and other men in suits. Even from her distant vantage point, she could see his smile.

She brushed a traitorous tear from her cheek. There was no question that he had treated her well. From the moment they stepped outside the church together, he had been more than a gentleman. But apparently even the best of gentlemen took advantage of people. She had foolishly thought of him as her white knight and had fallen in love with him. She had trusted him, but even though he had cared enough to find employment for her with his family, there wouldn't be a future with him. Not for her, anyway.

Spinning around, she took a long look at her room. Her one small suitcase sat unopened on the bed. She hadn't even had time to unpack. Her other small case was still in the car. Someone could send it to her, once she made it home.

She searched through a nightstand and found a piece of paper and a pen. Perching on the edge of the bed, she quickly wrote a note. When she finished, she left it on the bed and picked up her suitcase, hoping everyone would be busy outside. She planned to slip past the crowd of people, under the cover of darkness, and walk to the nearest town. After that she didn't have a plan and didn't know what might lie ahead. But it couldn't include Dev.

Chapter Ten

When the last of the cars had driven away and the guests were back in their cabins, Dev followed his family into the house. "Are you sure she's all right?" he asked Ellie in the entryway.

"A little stunned, I think, but mostly tired," she answered. "My guess is that she's sound asleep by now."

"She probably is." He quickly looked at his watch. It was late, but not too late to talk to his brothers. Everything had fallen into place. The sale of the Devil's Den was in progress and J.R. would soon be behind bars where he belonged. Even Carly's future was secure. It was time. He would check on Carly after he knew what his own future would be.

"Can we talk?" he asked his brothers. He was ready for this episode of his life to be over, no matter what the outcome. "It's important."

Trey joined him at the bottom of the stairs, rubbing his hands together. "I sense an announcement."

Chace walked over to them and punched the youngest Brannigan in the arm. "You're definitely a newlywed, baby brother. You seem to think everyone should get married."

"And you're what?" Trey asked. "An old married man?"

They sparred back and forth on the way to the office in the back of the house, but Dev paid no attention. He knew that once he told them about the morning of their father's death, all joking would end.

When each of them had taken a seat, a glass of bourbon in hand, Trey raised his glass in the air. "I'd like to propose a toast to our brother, Devon Brannigan, for putting an end to the Staton-Brannigan feud."

"Hear, hear," Chace said, raising his own glass in salute. "I guess we're celebrating, after all."

Dev could only stare into his glass. "Thanks," he said, looking up at each of them. "I only wish it could've been sooner."

"And there's still a trial to get through," Chace pointed out. "He'll be out on bail before the sun comes up."

"*If* he has the money," Trey reminded them, "or knows someone willing to put up the money. But something tells me that won't be a Brannigan."

"Or anyone who knows us," Chace said, laughing. "Let's hope he's sent up for a long time. Long enough to not pick up where he left off when he's released."

Trey snorted. "He should know by now that it won't do him any good. We've pretty much proven that, thanks to Dev."

"Not just me," Dev said. "From what I know, he'll have enough charges against him to keep him in jail until he's old and gray. We weren't the only ones wanting to see him caught, just the most determined."

Chace turned to Dev. "What are your plans? Back to your casino?"

Trey set his glass on the desk with a thud. "I sure hope not. We could use you here, Dev." He shook his head. "I said that wrong. We want you here, Dev. This is where you belong. If there's any way you can run the place from here—"

"Before we go any further, I need to…" Dev wasn't exactly sure what he should say. He had rehearsed this over and over in his mind so many times, he knew it by heart. But suddenly the wrong words were popping into his mind. What did he want to do? Confess his sins? Bare his soul? "I need to tell you something."

Chace looked at Trey, and then back again. "You have the floor, so to speak, and our attention."

Unable to sit, Dev got to his feet and walked to the window. He knew what lay beyond, outside in the darkness. His home. And he knew that doing this was risking ever being a part of it again.

Taking a deep breath, he turned to face his brothers. "I was responsible for Dad's heart attack."

Trey's eyebrows pulled together in a frown. "Wanna explain that?"

Chace was silent, but watching him closely.

"That's why I'm here," Dev admitted. "The morning of the attack, Dad and I had an argument."

"We all had arguments with him. He was a stubborn man," Chace said.

"It was worse than usual," Dev continued. "He was dead set on me going on to college. I didn't want to. I had other plans. Dad was furious."

"We're listening," Chace said, his face unreadable.

"I lost my temper and called him some names that no son should call his father," Dev admitted, fighting the memories of that morning as he told them. "I swore I'd leave the ranch and never return, rather than do what he wanted." He stopped, lowered his head and took a breath, unable to look at his brothers. "It's my fault. I take full blame for his heart attack."

When neither of his brothers spoke, he looked up at them, but they were merely watching him. He took a step forward, intending to leave. "I'll leave, if that's what you want."

"Sit down," Chace told him in a voice that was exactly like their father's.

Dev hesitated, thinking his brothers' anger was about to spill forth, but he took the closest chair and eased onto it. He had thought he was ready for anything, but he wasn't. He didn't want to leave. He wanted to stay. But there was no sense saying that now.

"Damn, Dev," Trey said, shifting his position on his own chair. "You been carryin' that around inside all these years?" When Dev nodded, Trey grunted. "Pretty damn foolish, considerin'."

"Considering?" Dev asked, looking from him to Chace.

"I guess we never told you," Chace answered. "We should have, but your visits were always so short, and I guess we never thought about it when you were here. We were too busy enjoying your company."

Dev had trouble swallowing. "Tell me what?"

"We found out years ago. The old man had had a serious heart condition for several years." Chace shook his head and blew out a breath. "Damn fool."

"And he had had another threat that morning, before he left the house, from the Statons. So if you want to blame someone, blame Jimmy Bob's old man," Trey explained.

"He was in a state of fury before you ever talked to him, Dev," Chace said, standing. He walked over and put his hand on Dev's shoulder. "He was a ripe candidate for a heart attack. You couldn't have known that. None of us did."

Trey pushed away from the desk and joined them. "If the stubborn old coot had only told us about his condition, things might have been different. Then again," he said with a shrug, "all of us have tempers. One of us would've eventually blown. It just happened that it was you, and at the wrong damn time."

"A heart condition," Dev said, still stunned by the news. If only he had known, even in the last few years. If only he had been brave enough to tell his brothers a long time ago. But if he really thought about it and admitted it to himself, he had enjoyed where his life had taken him after leaving the ranch. He just wished he had spent more time with his brothers when he had visited.

"Now what's this about leaving?" Chace asked. "You aren't planning on doing that, are you?"

"Only for a few days," he answered. "I have to finish up the sale, and I have an appointment with the eye doctor about this," he said, pointing to the patch over his left eye. "But I'll be back."

"Sale?" Trey asked.

Dev nodded and stood. "I'm selling the Devil's Den. Once the details are taken care of and I make certain the transition to the new owner will be smooth, I'll come back."

"For good?" Chace asked.

"For good."

Chace grabbed his hand to shake it, while Trey thumped him on the back and shouted, "Hot damn! The Brannigan brothers are back again!"

"If it's all right with you two, we'll celebrate tomorrow," Dev told them. "I need to check on Carly."

"Oh, sure," Trey said, sobering, but with a wink at Chace. "We'll see you in the morning."

Dev felt like running up the stairs, eager to tell Carly the news, but he confined his enthusiasm to taking them two at a time instead. At Carly's door he knocked lightly. "Carly? You still awake?"

She didn't answer. He was sure Ellie had said she'd gone to bed, and the house had been quiet when he left his brothers in the office. Needing to reassure himself that she was all right, he checked the door and found it unlocked, so he opened it and looked inside.

Even in the dark, with only the glow from the yard light shining in, he could see that the bed was empty. He flipped the light switch, bathing the room in brightness.

The empty bed was neatly made, just as it had been when they'd arrived. A folded piece of paper lay on the pillow, and he picked it up. But instead of opening and reading it, he searched the room, hoping to find her small suitcase, remembering that the other was probably still in the rental car.

He finally gave up, and the knot in his gut grew bigger. *She wouldn't have. She couldn't have.*

But her message in the note told the truth. In it she thanked him for his kindness and generosity and promised to repay him somehow as soon as she could.

She was gone.

Sinking to sit on the edge of the bed as he read it through again, he tried to make sense of what might have happened to cause her to leave. She made no mention of anything important, used no words of endearment. And that hurt him the most.

It was nonsense. Pure nonsense. And he would put a stop to it.

But a little voice whispered in his mind. *She's unstable, always running away when trouble comes knocking.*

No, that wasn't right. She was impulsive. She was trusting. But she damn sure wasn't unstable.

Crumpling the note in his hand, he stood and hurried out of the room. Other than walking, there wasn't any way she could have left the Triple B. He'd borrow one of the ranch's pickups and go find her. He'd put a stop to this craziness.

"Now do you remember why you don't like the dark?" Carly muttered to herself as she continued her walk down an obviously deserted road.

Too tired to take another step after what seemed like hours of walking, she stepped off the road, dropped her small suitcase and sank to the ground. She might be tired, but she was mad—steaming mad—at Dev and especially at herself.

Pressing her palms to her eyes, she shook her head. Would she never learn? She had fallen for another man who didn't return her affection, her love, and had used her for his own gain. She had figured out that Dev had helped her and kept her at the Devil's Den, hoping James would come looking for her. He probably had the police number on speed dial! The thought didn't cheer her and only threatened another wave of tears.

She had fallen hard this time. He had captured her heart, but he had done it with deceit, and she wouldn't go back to the ranch to ask for his help. She had too much of the Charpentier pride to do that.

If only she knew where she was going. And there was another of her flaws. She had left the ranch without being sure about which way to go and hadn't thought to take a flashlight. And Texas was big, especially with the dark, twinkling sky spread out endlessly above her.

All she wanted to know was if she was going in the right direction. They had driven through a town on the way from the airport to the ranch. She had been sure it wasn't far. But there wasn't even so much as a faint glow on the horizon to indicate there was even life in the area.

She'd done it again. Her impulsiveness had led her into a situation she couldn't control. She could only hope that someone—anyone—would come by to give her directions.

Several minutes passed as she continued to scold herself for her failings. Crying wouldn't do any good. It never had. Getting to her feet again, she picked up her bag and continued down the road.

She had heard nothing but the click-click of her shoes on the highway, so when she heard what sounded suspiciously like the engine of a vehicle, she stopped to listen more closely.

Sure enough, behind her she could see the approaching lights of something. Tugging at her shirt and rubbing at the dried remnants of earlier tears on her face, she stepped to the shoulder of the road.

As the vehicle approached, she could see it was a pickup truck and hoped the driver would stop so she could ask for directions. To her delight, it did slow down as it got nearer and eased to a stop beside her. But her delight turned to dismay when she recognized the driver.

"Nice night," he said, as if nothing had happened.

Furious that he would dare come after her, she ignored him and continued to walk.

"Come on, Carly, talk to me," he said, keeping the truck beside her.

She tipped her head up higher and remained silent. As far as she was concerned, he didn't deserve an answer. And anything he might say to her would probably be a lie. He was totally untrustworthy, even to someone as trusting as she was.

He pulled ahead of her slightly and stopped, obviously waiting until she caught up to him. Well, it didn't matter. He could keep trying until they reached the first town, even if it turned out to be twenty miles.

"Carly," he said, his voice low, but easily heard.

Her heartbeat kicked up a notch at the note of pleading in his voice. Oh, he knew how to sweet-talk her, and so had James. She had managed to ignore James's charm earlier, but she was finding that ignoring Dev's was much, much harder.

"Please," he said.

Her mouth went dry and she tried to swallow but couldn't. Oh, why did he have to make her feel this way? When she finally got over him—if she ever did—she would never fall in love again.

"This is crazy," she heard him mutter.

Crazy? Maybe. Safer for her heart? Definitely. No being impulsive this time. She'd keep her mouth shut. Tight.

The truck crept along next to her, then suddenly came to a stop. Dev leaned out the window on the passenger's side. "What do you think you're doing, Carly?"

Wheels started spinning in her head, and she smiled to herself. Stopping in her tracks, she turned to look at him, making sure her eyes were wide and she appeared as innocent as possible, before she asked.

"What are you doing out so late?"

He stared at her. His mouth opened, as if he was going to answer, but he immediately closed it again. Then he smiled the most devilish smile she had ever seen. So devilish—and sexy— that her knees threatened to buckle beneath her.

He moved back behind the steering wheel and, with a screech of rubber on the road, took off, leaving her staring at the taillights.

At first Dev chuckled, but as he slowed the truck to round the curve in the road, he began to laugh. He was still laughing past the curve when he pulled to the side of the road and cut his lights. She'd done it. She had turned the tables on him and answered his question with a question, exactly what he had done when they first met. And he deserved it. He had never been completely honest, and although there wasn't any way he could have, it wasn't fair. But it didn't mean he was going to let her walk out of his life without an explanation. Or even with an explanation, if he could help it.

He could tell by looking in the rearview mirror that she hadn't rounded the curve yet, and he hoped the sound of the truck's engine would bounce off the wall of rock to his right. With a flick of his wrist, he turned off the motor, thankful that he had grabbed a truck that wasn't noisy and hopeful that she didn't hear it.

Carefully opening the door, he stepped out onto the road and then eased the door shut. Walking as softly as possible so his footsteps wouldn't be heard, he stopped at the back of the truck and waited.

Sure enough, it wasn't long before he could see her coming around the bend in the road. Pushing away from the tailgate, he started walking to meet her. He knew the moment she saw him, because she stopped and took a step back. But apparently she decided that running back toward the ranch wasn't the best idea. Instead, she walked toward him. And she was mad.

At first he couldn't hear what she was shouting, but the closer they got to each other, the more he heard.

"…didn't tell me…should've known…kidnapped me…never trust…believe anything you tell me again. You're just as bad as James. Maybe even worse." She stopped in front of him and took a breath. "And you had the nerve to follow me, when I made it perfectly clear I was leaving."

"Are you finished?" he asked.

Her chin went up and her lips were set in a stubborn line. "Not hardly."

Before she could start in on him again, he grabbed her around her middle and tossed her onto his shoulder.

"Put me down!"

"That's what they all say," he said with a grin and turned for the truck.

"I mean it, Dev. I'll scream if you don't put me down."

She smacked him once with her small bag, and he chuckled. "Scream away," he said, holding tight to her wriggling body. "There's not another ranch for miles and, if you had asked, very little traffic on this road late at night."

"This is—it's…it's kidnapping!"

He was only a few feet from the truck, but he stopped in his tracks. "Why does everyone keep using that word?"

"Because that's what it is. And was."

He shook his head and sighed, picking up his steps again. "That's garbage, Carly. I just want to talk to you somewhere other than the middle of the road."

"I don't want to talk to you."

"Great," he said, stopping at the open tailgate of the truck. "You can listen."

He swung her from his shoulder and none too gently dumped her on the tailgate, prepared to grab her if she tried to run. Instead, she crossed her arms on her chest and glared at him, a sullen expression on her face.

"It really isn't safe out here at night by yourself," he told her.

She sniffed. "And when did my safety become a concern to you?"

Her verbal jab hurt far more than anything else could have. "That's not fair," he answered. "When haven't I been concerned about your safety? Name one time."

"You…I…" Instead of continuing, she dropped her head, only to jerk it up again. "Kidnappers often make certain their captives are safe. If they didn't— Well, you ought to know about that."

Brushing back a lock of her hair that had fallen across her cheek, he wondered how to break through this sudden burst of anger and resentment. He suspected he had hurt her, but for the life of him, he didn't know what he had done. "Didn't I take good care of you, from the second we stepped out of the church until I brought you to the Triple B? I made sure you had food and at least a few clothes. You had the run of the hotel and did pretty much what you wanted. Was that wrong?"

She shook her head, but she didn't look at him.

Tipping her chin up with his finger, he forced her to look at him. "I'm sorry, Carly, for anything I've done that's hurt you. It was never my intention to do anything like that."

"You used me," she whispered.

Even in the darkness of the Texas night, he could see the tears brimming in her eyes, and the sight made his heart ache with shame. But he didn't know how she had come to realize what had happened. "What makes you think so?"

Her hands, clasped in her lap, clenched and un-clenched. "You knew James would come after me when you took me from the church."

"I suppose I did," he admitted, dropping his hand.

Her gaze was intent, questioning, and she held his prisoner. "You were there to catch him, weren't you? Not as an old family friend, but as a man out to get revenge."

"Not revenge," he argued. "Justice. But, yes, I was there to see that he would pay for the things he had done. It wasn't revenge though."

"And if I hadn't stopped the ceremony, the church would have been swarming with police, just as the ranch was tonight."

"I suppose," he said, not eager to own up to something he now felt shame for even planning to do. Even though it had been less than two weeks, he couldn't remember exactly what he had hoped would happen at the wedding that didn't take place. He had given only a few moments of thought to what the wedding party and guests would think when J.R. was apprehended. His main objective had been to get the man who had ruined or attempted to ruin more people than Dev could count. He may not have gone about it in the best way, but he hadn't done it with the intention of hurting anyone.

"I did what I felt I had to do," he said. "And I kept you safe. I'll admit it looks bad. Maybe, at first, I used you, but—"

"I'm not saying you aren't a good man," she blurted.

"And I'm not saying I am. I didn't kidnap you, Carly," he said, sure of that one thing. He was suddenly sure of another. "And I didn't hold you prisoner in the hotel. What I did was make sure you were safe."

"But—"

"How many times did I offer to take you home or anywhere you wanted to go?" he asked.

She dipped her head, breaking the lock of their gazes, and the fight seemed to go out of her. "Several," she said in a quiet voice.

"Look at me, Carly." When she looked up, her eyes glistened with tears, and he knew he had to do everything he could to keep from losing her. He had to tell her the truth. If he hadn't been so unsure of his future and had trusted more in his family's love, he would have done it sooner.

Reaching for her hands, still clasped tightly in her lap, he held them. "When you went running up that aisle, I wasn't thinking about taking you to the Devil's Den. I wasn't thinking much of anything except helping a pretty lady in trouble and finding out a little more about why. To be honest, from the second you dumped J.R. in the church, you were my ace in the hole," he admitted with regret. "No matter where you went, I was pretty sure he would have eventually come to the Den, because he saw you leave with me."

"You acted on impulse?" she asked, brightening.

"Exactly. And that's something I don't do." He stopped, knowing he had to go on. But for the first time in his life, he was afraid of the outcome. "And neither is falling in love."

"Falling in love?"

"You weren't just my ace in the hole, Carly. You're my breath of fresh air, the person who makes me remember that there are other things in life besides work and staying the course. You're my queen of hearts."

"Wh-what do you mean?"

"I love you, Carly. I didn't plan it, but that's the way it is. I didn't know if I had anything to offer you. There was something I had to talk to my brothers about before I knew. I'll tell you about it someday, but I know now that I belong on the Triple B with my brothers. And I want to spend my life with you."

"I…I don't know what to say."

He tightened his grip on her hands, while his heart thundered in his chest. Her hesitation scared him. Bringing her hands to his lips, he kissed them. "Say you love me, too, Carly," he whispered.

She shook her head, sending his heart plummeting. "My judgment has always been so bad," she began, "and we both know how impulsive I am, but I do love you, Dev, and I can't imagine a life without you."

He couldn't have stopped his grin if his life had depended on it. "Then you'll marry me?"

When she nodded, he let out a whoop and released her hands to scoop her into his arms, kissing her until they were both breathless. Without putting her down, he grabbed her bag and carried her around the truck to set her inside, then climbed in after her.

"I'm going to love being your wife, Dev," she said as he started the engine.

Easing the truck forward, he made a U-turn in the middle of the road and punched the accelerator, eager to get back to the ranch. "And I'm going to love having you as my wife."

Slipping her hand in his, she smiled. "I can't wait to be a real member of the Brannigan family. But I have one question."

"What's that?" he asked, knowing his family would be just as pleased when they heard the news. Especially Trey.

"Will I still have a job?"

He glanced at her, sitting beside him, and couldn't help laughing. "You'll still have the job," he said, sobering, "and you can start as soon as we get back from a long, long honeymoon."

Epilogue

"Don't I know you?" the plump, middle-aged woman asked, leaning close to study him.

Dev glanced at Carly beside him in the reception line and patted the woman's hand. "I don't believe we've met," he said, knowing full well they had. But without his eye patch, which had been removed several months before, the woman who had sat next to him at the wedding-that-wasn't obviously didn't remember him.

"You look so familiar…" She continued to stare at him as he released her hand and she moved on to Carly, who quickly introduced them.

"I like this one better," the woman said to his new bride in a conspiratorial voice. "Don't let him get away."

Laughing, Carly looked up at Dev. "Oh, I won't do that."

Since returning to Baton Rouge in early September so Carly could work on finalizing the wedding plans, Dev had learned what it meant to have a heart swell with pride. It seemed as though everyone in the city knew her and loved her. But they could never love her as much as he did. And that love grew more each day that passed.

Leaning close to Carly, his lips brushed her cheek. "When can we get out of here?" he whispered so no one would hear.

Her eyes widened, but sparkled with mischief. "We still have to cut the cake. Then there's the toasts and mingling and dancing and—"

"The honeymoon," he said, grinning.

"Is that all you can think about?" she asked, adding a pout he knew was as phony as J.R. Staton.

"Pretty much," he answered, hoping he looked serious and knowing she was looking forward to it as much as he was. Looking around, he noticed that the line of guests waiting to congratulate and wish them well had disappeared. "It won't be long now," he teased his bride.

She slipped her arm through his and tugged him away from their spot near the door. "Then let's get this done."

He laughed at her enthusiasm, and they joined his family, who had gathered on the other side of the crowded room.

"Are you feeling all right?" Carly asked Meg. "Do you need to sit down?"

Arching her back and sighing, Meg smiled. "I'm fine, but I think it's time to find a place to sit. It was a beautiful wedding, Carly, and you're so sweet to have Ellie and me as your bridesmaids."

Carly wrapped her arms around her, giving her a sisterly hug. "I wouldn't have anyone else. We're family. Prissy wasn't so pleased about it," she added with a giggle, "and even though I'm ever so thankful for her poor judgment where James was concerned, asking her to help serve the cake was as generous as I could be."

"Speaking of Prissy and cake," Dev said, taking her hand and giving it a squeeze, "she's waving us over to the table."

Carly returned the squeeze as they made their way to the gaily decorated table where the enormous cake sat waiting for the honors. "Where are Chace and Ellie?" she asked, searching the room.

Dev took the cake knife from Carly's former best friend and pointed in the direction of his oldest brother. "Over there," he answered, and handed her the knife.

"Oh, he has one of the babies!"

"And Ellie has the other." He placed his hand over hers as instructed and nodded in his sister-in-law's direction. "And as soon as we board the cruise ship, we'll start working on having our own," he whispered.

She looked up at him, her eyes filled with desire and excitement. "I can't wait."

His blood warmed and his body reacted. "Then let's get this cake cut." He felt as if he were on hold and his life would start again as soon as the festivities were over. In a sense it was true. Even though they had said their I do's, and Carly was officially and legally Mrs. Devon Brannigan, he wouldn't feel married until they were alone. That's what he looked forward to the most. Just having Carly to himself. Dev wouldn't have it any other way. He even told Chace so when his brother told him he was looking a bit restless.

"In a hurry to get the honeymoon started?" Chace joked and looked down at the bundle he was holding. "You know that kind of thing results in this, don't you?"

Dev peeled back the edge of the blue blanket and peered down at the dark-haired infant, sleeping peacefully in his father's arms. "Looks good to me," he answered.

Chace's expression was a portrait in love. "It is. And to think that Ellie and I have been doubly blessed, well, it's hard to believe. Keeps me awake nights sometimes."

As Carly walked up to join them, Dev slipped his arm around her and held her close. "I hope I'm even half as lucky as you, big brother."

"Mom always said you had the Devil's luck," Chace reminded him. "Triplets, maybe?"

"Heaven forbid!" Carly cried. "Dev, he hasn't jinxed us, has he?"

Dev looked down at her, her face radiant with love, and leaned down to kiss her. "The Brannigans don't jinx each other," he said, brushing his lips against hers.

Chace cleared his throat. "Uh, Dev?"

Straightening, Dev found himself face-to-face with the minister who had performed the ceremony. "Just kissing my bride, Reverend," he said, offering his hand. "I think that's customary?"

Reverend McNabney smiled and shook his hand. "Oh, yes, quite customary. In fact, I encourage it."

"Thank you for a wonderful ceremony," Carly said.

"You're always welcome, Carly," the minister replied, his eyes twinkling. "I'm especially pleased that you made it all the way through *this* ceremony."

Dev was grateful the reverend had a sense of humor, and he gave Carly a loving hug as they laughed at the man's joke. He had been uncertain when Carly had first insisted their wedding take place at the same church where she had nearly married J.R. But she had assured him that no one would think anything of it. He realized that he didn't care where they held the wedding, just as long as they had one. And he wouldn't deprive her of sharing the moment with her family and friends, especially since her new home would be on the Triple B.

When the minister had wished Dev and Carly well and gone to speak to some of the other guests, Dev turned to Chace. "All finished with the move into your new house?"

Chace nodded. "And it wasn't easy with these little guys, but Ellie hung the last of the pictures the day before we left for here. You'll only have to share the main house with Trey and Meg until your house is finished."

"If we're lucky, that'll be done by the time we get back from the Caribbean." Dev looked at Carly. "We ought to be moved in just in time for Thanksgiving."

"I can't wait," she answered, her eyes shining with excitement. "And then we'll have Christmas with all the family. That's what I'm really looking forward to doing."

"You may think otherwise," Dev teased her, "with so many of us now." Carly's mother and new stepfather had also been invited to the ranch to share the holiday. But he, too, was excited at the prospect of the Brannigan family Christmas. It had been too many years since he had spent the holiday with his brothers.

His life was definitely on the upswing. With J.R. serving time for fraud and other crimes, the Brannigan family could finally breathe easy. For Dev it was a longtime dream coming true.

Their lives wouldn't be a pat hand, but with Carly at his side, along with the rest of the Brannigan family, he knew that whatever happened, the Brannigans and their kin would prosper in true Brannigan style.

* * * * *

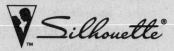

HARLEQUIN *Presents*

Royal Brides

The Scorsolini Princes:
proud rulers and passionate lovers
who need convenient wives!

Welcome to this brand-new miniseries,
set in glamorous and exotic places—it's
a world filled with passion, romance and royals!

Don't miss this new trilogy by

Lucy Monroe

THE PRINCE'S VIRGIN WIFE
May 2006
HIS ROYAL LOVE-CHILD
June 2006
THE SCORSOLINI MARRIAGE BARGAIN
July 2006

SILHOUETTE *Romance*®

COMING NEXT MONTH

#1814 THAT OLD FEELING—Cara Colter

Accustomed to taking risks, Brandy King wants to bolt when
her father asks her to help widower Clint McPherson through his
emotional turmoil. Now this daredevil woman faces her greatest
challenge—how to handle all the old feelings when she's reunited
with this man who once broke her young heart….

#1815 SOMETHING'S GOTTA GIVE—Teresa Southwick

The weird phone calls and mysterious pop-up messages shook
Jamie Gibson. But her new bodyguard has her definitely on edge.
Sexy, dedicated Sam Brimstone has promised to keep her safe and
then be gone. But trapped between the intense attraction she feels
for Sam and the threat of an unknown stalker, Jamie knows that
something's gotta give….

#1816 SISTER SWAP—Lilian Darcy

Can identical twins really swap places? Singer Roxanna Madison
tries to adopt some of her sister's meeker characteristics for an
important business trip to Italy. But her new boss, the gorgeous
Gino di Bartelli, and his motherless child have her own heart and
voice threatening to bubble to the surface.

#1817 MADE-TO-ORDER WIFE—Judith McWilliams

Billionaire Max Sheridan had assumed the etiquette expert he hired
would be a dowdy grandmother. Instead, the beautifully dynamic
Jessie Martinelli has his orderly mind turning from politeness to
more, well, complicated matters of the heart. Is this expert about
to give him a lesson in love?

SRCNM0406